AF254525

Bird Skeletons and Other Stories

Gabriela Torres Cuerva

BIRD SKELETONS
AND OTHER STORIES

BIRD SKELETONS
AND OTHER STORIES

GABRIELA TORRES CUERVA

You're Going to Die

There's not much time, no more than an hour. I know you. I can tell the end is near. 60 minutes. The swollen veins of your hands remind me of the crab legs that Susan Sontag talked about. They're cold. The vessels through which blood flows feel frozen, barely palpitating. Blood flows, stops, flows, and stops. You're a river, my love, about to become still amongst bramble, moss, and fish, resistant to the sterile water. Your lips, a diabolic expression that denotes how quick you will become a grain of sand once you leave the water. One hour. From anguish comes precision. What the fuck has time become now? I don't do anything except think too much about shit. With everything and your hate, I prefer your company instead of these thoughts. I'm relieved to be in this room with you and looking out the window bothers me. That's where risk is. Here it's calm.

We can't bet like we used to anymore: if I won, I'd get on top of you and I'd cum twice if I was lucky; if you won, I'd lay down in the angelical missionary position. Both dominatrix exercises were practiced dozens of times. Wild dogs. We never liked to be submissive, right? But the almost-dead don't fuck. They don't even bet. Your mind might have opened a bit so that some light could shine in, a condor that you'd reveal in your aphorisms, the stroll on the port of Veracruz when we got overcome by desire and didn't have any intention to deny it. The only thing that entered through that space was the command that you dared to give me:

"They're gonna get you. Leave."

You were telling me to run, motherfucker. I remember your exact words while I think about a vulture licking its lips for your brains.

"Get out of here. Today."

Just like that. Get out. What balls to tell me to go to hell, when you were the one who had put me in the hands of the most esteemed narco of the world. The guy that everyone looks down upon, admires, hates. The one who's Sinaloan eyes bulge, his hands and head trickle with blood. If it hadn't been for you, he would've never gotten near me.

You're probably fucked up by now, but in that moment, you were a son of a bitch. Just a tiny excuse was enough to send what we had to hell. The good was erased from your mind and you decided to throw me into the fire. To take your feet out of black water and leave me to die, even though you thought you were saving yourself. That made you strong. You felt good, with a manageable treatment, an optimistic prognosis. Your expectation was to live and mine was to stay with you. Nemesis is the punishment for Hubris, dear: mere retributive justice. You exaggerated your confidence in yourself, you shunned me from your life, because in the end you were going to save yourself. And now, beautiful, you'll die when I was supposed to be the dead onehated. I'm afraid, I won't say I'm not. I am a coward. With El Chapo inside and out, at any moment they'll catch me. But I'm still alive, and you'll soon be dead. They always say hindsight is 20/20.

And all of this because of your urologist, Dr. Williams. What was the point of him knowing that I was a ghost writer, if his job was to take care of his patient: you. In the waiting room I read an essay by Sontag about language of the sickly: that impenetrable world for everyone else. You both left the office. I hadn't decided to turn the magazine page with discretion, fold it with care and throw it in my backpack when I saw you arrive. He patted your back while directing you to the lady in reception so you could pay the one thousand pesos you owed. He then came back to me and asked:

"So, you write for others?"

I gave him my card. He told me he'd give me a call. I always had the intention to write a story. That's what everyone says. He was dying (that's how he said it) to have a book about his life. Now I think about the wickedness of common words. The man was happy. A book to show off his bachelor's from the United States, narrate his childhood in Chiapas... above all, he loved the idea of delivering a testimony of his achievements to his professional enemies and the friends who politely hated him. Some, according to him, had been jealous of him for ages, since he had gotten to a luxurious building and in little time became a partner of the owners after investing in a good part of the property.

"I've experienced so many things, Gabriela, and you wouldn't believe it. It's been hard, but very satisfying," he said, looking at my card. "You'll get my call soon."

I thanked you for the new client. Dr. Williams had the look of being prompt with his payments. I loved getting a good advance. I hugged you tightly and we went to dinner. The bets started after my tequila and your whiskey. If Dr. Williams had talked to me within a week, I'd put on the most detestable lingerie: fishnets with an opening in the crotch. I always thought it was a medieval piece of clothing, prudish. Its design still seems unfortunate to me: able to shut down even the horniest guy, but you loved it. My bet was that if he didn't call in that amount of time, you'd get on top of me and resist until I had two orgasms. Whoever lost got double the punishment. It was something like having a piggy bank, saving pleasures. You never know when you're going to need them.

Dr. Williams' enthusiastic voice rang. I had to put on the insufferable piece of clothing. You just had your exams done and there was optimism, hope with respect to the results. A good mood is the best aphrodisiac. The night treated us well.

As soon as you started your treatment, I started my sessions with Williams. We met on Saturdays, because he didn't have as many patients to see and it was easier to concentrate.

For a couple of weeks, it went a lot like this: he spoke, I recorded, and then I'd write. I covered the first years of a small, curious Williams, with almost red, very curly hair, inclined to get himself in dangerous circumstances. Right there, at about page 30, was when he dropped the bomb that would lead us – you and I – and Mr. Williams, to a better life:

"I'm going to tell you something. Promise me that what you hear won't leave this room. Its very sensitive information and could put us both at risk."

"Whatever you say stays between us. And in your book, of course."

I supposed that he was referring to what I was going to write about him. Clients like to protect themselves. They always have this feeling their life has unique, valuable details. When they start to see their life played out in pages, they fear that someone may want to take over their story.

"Have you heard of el Chapo Guzmán?"

He waited to see my reaction. I didn't know what to say. It was discomforting to see his expecting face, urged to get something out of me.

"The thing is that this doctor," he adjusted the neck of his tie as a sign of pride, "is his urologist."

The doctor wanted me to write the anecdote in his book. That's what it was all about.

"I spoke to him about you. About ten years ago his nephew started to write his biography, but they killed him in a brawl, so the book was never finished. He finds the story romantic, written with old-fashioned innocence. El Chapo isn't young nor old, 56, but in newspapers they make him out to be older. Could you imagine? Thank God I'm not famous, with all those years and life tightening his throat. He's sure that he'll remain healthy," he adjusted his tie again, "but death pursues him. That chases him, that's why he asked his applied, studious nephew for the esteemed book. He wants people to know where he comes from. That way he can live his life in peace. Do you think el Chapo is anguished?"

The doctor spoke on without stopping. He said a lot of things. Even if I trembled, I couldn't feel it. The only thing that crossed my mind was the beautiful metafiction: client making another client, one story about the other. Literature, in essence. I thought about something else. I'll confess to you now, since when you told me to run, we couldn't even talk. Fury overtakes everything. But today there isn't enough time to lie, exactly what el Chapo wanted to do with his life in the fucking book. I thought about not letting it go. I never let a project go. You've always said that I do it for money. Maybe. One must live off of something and I write.

From night to the morning, the new client was on my agenda. I didn't tell you. It isn't easy going around screaming about something this size. Had you told me no, I would've still done it. You know me.

El Chapo had presented the first symptoms of prostate cancer a few months ago, when Dr. Williams was called by his representative, some José María. The same one that came by the office for me to take me to see the man whose name makes most people tremble, the man who resides in the highest-level security prison in Puente Grande. You were in such a bad mood to return to the hospital. Even though now you doubt it, I kept quiet too, to not bother that difficult discipline of yours that made you a sack of nerves. I could already see you screaming: "You're only in it for the money!" Well, no, I have feelings.

The doctor, as the good person he was, was excited. The cancer had been localized on time and that made him proud.

"That I can't put in the book, Gabriela. You understand. It's our secret."

It moves me to think now of his clean face, free of worries. After a meeting in which we arrived at page 52, they came to the hospital looking for me in a black pick-up truck parked in the F4 parking space, the same one as always. Until the last afternoon, I always would go there with open-toed shoes without platforms. I wore just two articles of clothing on top of my underwear, no kind of accessories. Not even the watch or the silver ring that you say I stole when you told me to go fuck myself. It was already mine, beast! A man descended from each side, they greeted me with courtesy, they showed me where I could sit in the back seat (sometimes on the left side). They didn't say a word during the entire 40 minutes of the ride. The man to my side, the "Licenciado", a handsome, angular-faced man, was the key piece of that chess game: I registered his incisive glance at my hands. I usually move anxiously when I feel worried or nervous, like now, when I sense a normal heartbeat rhythm coming from the device without needing to turn around. And if you get saved, I wonder, what the fuck will happen if you get saved.

One time a journalist friend told me that el Chapo had a split personality, what some people would call *borderline* personality disorder. These people embellish with Freudian allusions the confusion between the rejection of real danger and the fear of discovering it. I remembered him as he entered. The access to the Puente Grande prison was almost as simple as the cooking oil company's entrance, the same one I used to write for once a week for its fiftieth anniversary. They asked me for my ID, they passed their metal detector from head to tie, and told me to take off my shoes. With a signal from the Licenciado, we entered a long hallway, a few fences, a metal door, stairs, until we got to Chapo Guzmán's door. I learned quick: I didn't take a step until they told me to. More than a cell, the space was a simple apartment with all the necessities. Television, a couple of couches, a bar with two metal stools, a table with magazines. In a black leather seat my client, who stood up, made an assuring movement as if he wanted to affirm his feet into the ground. He spoke about something with el Licenciado, a couple of words. Finally, he spoke to me:

"Do you know how to write or have you come to die with me?"

I felt my tense smile, stupid.

"Dr. Williams spoke highly of your work. He saved me from dying and now I can't get rid of him. Can I trust you?"

I supposed, now in a calmer mental state, that he referred to my work as a narrator. I said yes. I insisted on discretion, taking care to not specify him, but rather to show my confidentiality policy that I have with other authors. He made a strange face, a gesture where his eyes and forehead joined together for one sole expression: doubtful.

"They're the lives of the authors I write about, that's why I call them that."

"Take a seat, Gabriela. I don't like really tall women."

Someone that I didn't look at brought over a seat. We didn't look eye to eye. He took his place on the couch and sat in the corner from where I was sitting. An isosceles triangle was formed between the table, Mr. Guzmán, and I. That's how I began to call him, by mere intuition. It seemed, by the look of his brow, that I hit the nail on the head.

The Licenciado assigned me a computer, set aside the magazines, and gave me two recommendations. His bearded face stuck his eyes on me as he spoke:

"You can't record audio. You can't save any files on a USB either."

I couldn't do any of that since they'd taken everything from me. Finally, he told me that Dr. Williams would be in charge of letting me know what days and hours I had to work. That caught my attention and it would intrigue me even more when Dr. Williams wasn't there to tell me what was going on. When metafiction became a tunnel of blood in the doctor's memory-filled head and he'd never have the possibility of making his colleagues burn with envy at his book's publication.

The computer was old, but in flawless condition. Meanwhile el Chapo tended to his beard, as if he wanted to identify something strange. Then he rummaged through his right ear with a finger. I saw it all without turning to see it directly, thanks to this stupid ability to observe without others noticing.

I went exactly ten times to Puente Grande. My calendar reflects that faithfully: Dr. Williams let me know the day and the time. I have the sensation that it was raining with the Licenciado told me, upon returning to the building where Dr. Williams worked, that they would be looking for me. It's blurry. I barely remember a comment the chofer made in relation to the flooded street. Licenciado's gesture was the same as the gesture he made to me the first afternoon, when I didn't know anything about el Chapo and you and I were still together. Everything could have stopped that day in the office if you hadn't fucked with the destiny of your writer girlfriend by recommending her. He didn't look at my hands, but he studied my reaction: his pistol cannon-like eyes stuck on my forehead. I didn't register any of it in the moment, just as I won't prove your death until you're dust in the dust. I understood the change of signal: Dr. Williams wouldn't be the day and time messenger for when el Chapo could see me anymore. I was calm again: without fear, without trepidation.

The last time I saw Dr. Williams you were hospitalized for a relapse. You had a burning fever all night and by dawn, after having drained the cold compress resources, I took you to the hospital. The doctor dictated by phone the order that you'd have exams done and take pain killers. He appeared with his impeccable coat and a smile on his face. "Good news," he said, but his voice said the opposite. You just needed hydration, according to him. You were already going downhill and maybe Dr. Williams' gimmick was to make you feel the contrary, or he had a feeling of what was coming for him and he decided to take down the black birds with one big slap. He looked exultant, strange. He seemed anxious for the launch of his book. He distracted us with that. It was that damn outpour of faith and enthusiasm that made me fall. Damn doctor. That night I decided to tell you about el Chapo. You didn't say a word to me until the next day at home when you told me to get out.

Not even a week passed when the scandal unfolded. The news channels wouldn't talk about anything else. Dr. Williams was found in his car with two gunshots to the forehead. The last anecdote that I managed to write was the day stroll he took with his wife, under an orange, extreme sunset on the tip of bursting. The doctor got all poetic to describe the details. Soon a squirrel crossed the avenue and was run over by a car. His wife yelled and blamed him for remaining unperturbed after seeing the poor luck of a living being.

I finally trembled and got caught up in fear. I shut off my phone for hours. Later I turned it on to see if there were any calls, then I turned it off again. "Why the doctor," you would've asked me if you had talked to me still. And I'd be dumbfounded, stupid in the face of an inexplicable act. What the fuck happened? Now I think you would've just saved that question and thrown a direct one:

"How stupid are you. You're next. As far as I'm concerned, die alone."

I dreamed of the headline in the newspaper. "Chapo Guzmán's doctor assassinated because of suspected links to narcotrafficking".

The Licenciado didn't call anymore. There were three versions of el Chapo's escape. In a dirty laundry car taken by custodians to the clearance of the prison. Dressed as a woman. Or a police officer. Why the hell does it matter? I've thought a lot about the geography of the place: the door, the fence, the guard asking me to take off my shoes, Chapo's question when we met. The dead doctor. Afterwards, his escape. A disconnected, confusing map. One thing obviously had something to do with the other, but that's how it happened.

I entertain myself dreaming about the news when I die. Its like eating your nails and pulling your hair. It'd give you pleasure to know I'm scared. The Licenciado said that they'd come for me. It sounds stupid, unreal to me. He said it with that way he stares with his eyes. El Chapo is out and his people are out to save him, maybe I'm not even in his plans. With luck, care, I may be able to live and nobody will read: "Ghost writer dead because of suspected links…"

Sontag defines death as a thin thread where we all recognize each other. Today the hospital told me you have little time left. I'm not to blame for having my number in your file. The machine and the bustle of the nurses tell me you're going to die. The bets are done. I might die, but now I'm alive watching you leave. If we had bet, the picture would be clear. On top of you in euphoria. You squeezing my buttcheeks. And the unused black claw thrown out over there, with the ridiculous hole through which life slips away.

Cuts

As if it rose from the mouth of a pale, light expands outward and everything is made bigger. Now I think it was worth the effort having worked so much to get a few days of vacation. Pablo is calm since the iguana ordeal. It was almost a lizard with its ample chin and pale scale on its head. Fascinated by how quick he could climb and by the spikes behind his neck, he finally stopped grumbling and grips my hand tightly. He doesn't ask me for a knife anymore, even though that doesn't mean I should shout for joy. At least he forgets in that moment that his hand seems to tremble in mine. He must feel fear – it isn't common to feel something like that from him – at the same time his marveled eyes scan the place. He does like that, not like the nautical rigs from the Boat Museum, where boats made of all kinds of sizes and materials ended up making him queasy and put him in a terrible mood. He's fine now, although he's still insisting on the knife.

We took our place in the boat. Many people waited their turn; the vacation season was perfect for a place with lots of sun, green, and a little bit of adventure. Everybody was wearing bermudas and shirts appropriate for the situation; only Pablo and I didn't fit in. Some looked at us like we were crazy, I guess it seemed unnatural that you'd dare to wear boots, windbreakers, and long pants. As it tends to happen, people blocked the way in search of places at the front of the boat; only a couple of people fit at a time and the rest dispersed for the rest of the seats. Pablo and I were entertained, maybe with the hustle and bustle of the people, when suddenly, a yellow bird landed on a railing of the boat. I got uncomfortable. Colors so close are always a problem, and those lively feathers and everything that emits an intense brightness. As a boy I had to avoid putting him close to lamps and flashlights; the consequences could be terrible. The thing that can make him go out of control is light in movement, and that bird, colorful and graceful, did not seem to be in a hurry to take flight. "A *dendroica*," said someone who happened to know ornithology, there's always one. Just a couple of seconds were all that was needed. Pablo wielded the knife and tried to hunt it; when he saw it disappear with a furious flutter his face took on a grim, sinister look. I took the precaution of holding him with my arms around his hip as I always do. We struggled for a while; the struggle always seems like a kind of eternity between us. In the end, he let me put away the knife with the condition that he'd get it back before we left the boat. As soon as we went on our way, he asked me for it. I ignored it while I could; the iguana show helped him keep calm, after – as it tends to happen – he won me over with his serious kid face, with his eyebrows slightly raised. I gave in, and when I did, I asked him to behave. I spoke to him about the wonders of having two days to ourselves and I begged him to behave in accordance with the circumstances. He put it in between his legs and every now and then would put his hands there and tightened his thighs.

The noise of the motor is rhythmic, as if to a metronome. A part of stomach is seen from the shirt of the man sitting in front of us; he caresses it every now and then and leaves his hand there, as if he could feel it pulsate. Pablo was looking too intently and I had to punish him. You're not supposed to stare at anybody. People who stare aren't well regarded by most people. These are things I tell him frequently. The man seems to be a nice guy, someone you can trust. He loves natural spectacles and feels happy to be there; he proclaims it with pride to the girl and the woman that accompany him, who wear a similar wardrobe: a white, sailor-like shirt with blue borders and marine blue shorts. I'm not one to look head to toe, even less with I have Pablo next to me; I can barely deal with him to be entertaining myself with gossip, but I couldn't help but look at their socks. Pink and white squares. The desire of the man to record until the last event of the tour with his camera is very noticeable. The continuous flashes bother Pablo. He begins to make noises with his mouth. He also starts hitting his hand with a fist repeatedly.

I assumed that it would happen to him as soon as we had entered exotic territories, when other animals came to the shore to drink or to snoop around, instigated by the noise of the engine. But Pablo began to scratch behind his ears like when he gets nervous, then started scratching his head as if something stung him. He put his hands between his legs where he kept the knife. He knew that he couldn't use it, and if I gave it to him it was only so that he could be at peace. The view, the types of birds and vegetation recited by the boat driver seemed to catch his attention, at least enough to not worry about him so much. The names of the mangroves made him laugh: botoncillo, bobo, prieto. He repeated them two or three times and with each one, he laughed again. The man with the camera began to laugh too, with every new reference, while he looked to Pablo in hopes of some signs of mutual understanding. When he didn't get any reaction from Pablo, he stopped doing it and continued taking pictures. I hated that he had to do so much of the same, so many lights and flashes. He showed a picture to one of the people with him who celebrated with laughter. That did make them different: while the woman covered her mouth, the girl opened hers in exaggeration. They stopped laughing at the same time as if they had agreed upon it.

While we passed through the narrow channel of the swamp, the branches scratch the arms of those who, despite having heard the instructions not to, stick them out of the boat anyways. The boat driver said it at the beginning of the tour and repeats it when the trail of water begins to narrow. Pablo draws waves in the water; sometimes he puts his palms against the waves that form as the boat advances. At first, he's startled and touches his arms. I know him, he can't believe that those twisted trees have been able to touch him. He insults them, wishes them the worst, hoping that the water swallows them mercilessly and that only a few of their miserable humid leaves remain upon the swampy ground. That they die, that all the stupid mangroves disappear from this world. They're only good for scratching people. I don't remember his exact words, but I do remember the meaning. I don't try to calm him down; at this point I've come to understand a fair dimension of his attitude: my intentions would only stimulate him more. While he curses, he doesn't stop playing with his forearm. He's always had delicate skin, that kind of skin where any scratch would look worse than it is. Two large scratches form an elongated X. There's no blood, but the regular red appearance of most scratches. I make a comment about the free tattoo, trying to be lighthearted. He looks at me enraged, with those green lights in his pupils, the same ones that anticipate misfortunes. The man starts to calm him down. That is a problem.

Everything would've been fine had he stayed in his place, calm before the quotidian act of a child's tantrum, but no, with a certain kind of effort he got close to Pablo and touched his shoulder while he told him things about resignation and encouragement. Until that point all was calm, before my worried eyes and the compassionate looks of the woman and the girl who didn't miss any details of his attempt to calm Pablo down. Then it happened. Pablo, who kept his hands between his legs again, took out the knife with utmost care and put it for a few moments on the side of the boat. Ignoring the man, he started to carve marks into the metal surface of the boat: two crosses like the one on his arm. I told him to cut it out and the girl, in total solidarity with what was going on, asked me to leave him alone as if she were already an adult. That was when I lost my rhythm: I turned around to look at her and when I did, I heard the scream. I can't be sure. The cut wasn't so deep, but it was deep enough so that the man wouldn't be able to save his hand. I tried to address his anger like any mother would, to apologize or say some bullshit that you say in these cases, but a known weight on my neck forced me to look down. I saw Pablo's fat shoes, one on top of the other after uncrossing his feet and change sides multiple times.

The girl squeals, a little bit hysterical. Both do: the woman and her. I ask about the wound and the three of them, now protected with one another, kept quiet and respond with a contemptuous look. The density of silence intensifies. The other tourists say things amongst themselves, they point me out, accuse mothers like me, kids that are a lost cause, they disapprove what happened moving their head and establish universal theories. The environment on the boat becomes insufferable. I want to fly like the yellow bird or reach the top of a tree with the quickness of an iguana. I hate Pablo, I always hate him in these cases. An infinite grudge burns my throat and keeps me from saying a word. Again, I feel the pressure on my neck, the desire to keep my head down. I entertain myself in the bluish-green water. I remember the paper boats my dad used to make. I liked to make them sink, ruin them when they made contact with the water. Maybe I felt some kind of superiority when I did it. A sensation of power.

Before getting to the last part of the route, the visual field widens again. The man has wrapped a cloth around his hand and mutters nonstop with the girl and the woman. I don't listen to what they say anymore. I'm concentrated on the buzz of the motor. Everything is enormous. A crocodile sunbathes. The surface of its great animality looks dry, in total paradox with the humidity in which it lies. I'm not sure if Pablo sees it. I have the knife in my power once again. I feel it, Pablo glances at it every now and then. His fingers trace the scratch on his forearm. What I can affirm is that he has that unbearable smile. That foolish, stupid paper smile.

Bird Skeletons

That way of speaking isn't normal. Just three or four words. Incompatible. One twisted in with another. A type of vibration stays in the air when he spits out the last syllable. The air in the room gets tense. Its his anger that floats in the air: the frustration of not being able to communicate as fast as before when we read in bed for hours and he was full of opinions. We'd always end up on top of each other. Now his strength has diminished: Ruly's body isn't the same anymore, but mine is still the same. He rubs his hands on the shirt he uses as pajamas with the frenetic intention of an assassin who wants to erase his digital fingerprints. I can only see him out the corner of my eye: his eyes have changed so much that it is hard work looking at them for more than a couple of seconds.

The two of us are in bed, supporting ourselves on our pillows. We usually read aloud on that blessed thing. The custom has been to alternate who reads. Lately, the duty has been mine: it is hard for him to say one sentence with the same breath. We recently finished an excerpt of *El cochero extraordinario*: the conversation in Soho between absolute believers and skeptics without a cure. One of them wields a bottle angrily, which if it were a sword in efforts to defend his posture in respect to the impossibility of being absolutely certain about something. It is at that point when Ruly tries to make a gesture, imitating the character: he raises his hand energetically, but hesitates in a strengthless exposition. That breaks him and tears him to pieces. I show indifference before his rage. The littlest gesture could give me away. How can I tell him?

Some months ago, Ruly and I made a decision. He had two years to live together, even though it seems like 100 or 1,000. Our relationship was a lot like many others that work well, without song and dance. We always gave dialogue priority, supply enough blood to that river. Talking was our favorite virtue. We decided. And we were wrong. When I realized it, I decided again: to save myself. It was too late to confess and every time it got even later: paths closed and between us was an abyss. I wanted to confess. Later I regretted wanting to do it. I kept silent. Now there's nothing to do.

We decided together. We committed to something significant. That swallowing of thick saliva in which you decide to take a different route than the habitual one happened at a friends meeting. Being born in the 60's and 70's, inhabitants of a city that's still a town, now immense and out of control, the different anecdotes from our childhoods coincided: mom killing a hen in front of us to later make chicken soup, raw milk that arrived to our houses in huge metallic barrels. All these almost-mythical images recreated the lives of these happy, fat children, dying to eat this or that. The leap in the chronology was imminent. Now with grown-up children of our own, except Ruly and I, we got bitter thinking about the consequences for the new generation versus the nonchalant old people seeing David Bowie, swallowing serrano ham and Iberian chorizo with their rounds of whiskies, tequilas, and mezcales.

I don't know when we started to talk about the brutality with which they killed animals to be consumed by human beasts. That's the point where you start to hate yourself a little. The drinks distorted the vision of things; now I can see it in the light of nostalgia for what we were. We're getting old, someone said. It was true. In favor of a fresh and healthy humanity, for our old bodies and even as a tribute to the elderly parents, we decided to raise a flag that said *We can be heroes for ever and ever* and take a step towards food culture that was congruent with reality.

And so, it was so easy, the path in which Ruly and I climbed up in a single, deadly jump, from a carnivorous existence to a vegan one, whose number one belief is to not consume any food made from animals. We got home, drunk and happy, at three o'clock in the morning. We cursed against the obtuse vision that we had had up until that point; excited, we stuck almost all the contents of the fridge in bags. We hopped into bed and stared at the computer screen until dawn, reading articles about the topic. The dark hand of health gave us the first grip on our throats. The damage was done.

The first couple of days were difficult. Being that we were used to eating meat everyday for decades, we changed our diets to various legumes and a combination of soy and cereal. We quit, according to the strict rules of veganism, even milk, eggs, and honey. The euphoria of the first night was diluted into a persistent aroma of delicious vegetables at the beginning but became unbearable afterwards. Everything was smooth, easy to digest; however, our stomachs were always half full and never completely satisfied.

When I'd go grocery shopping, I couldn't stop drooling over the ham and turkey sandwiches on the posters. I felt a deep envy for people that filled their shopping carts with meat products. I began to feel weak and I'm sure Ruly did too; maybe because we were committed to our paired agreement, neither one of us dared to raise our voices in favor of a new proposal. It had to do something with a matter of honor. Just thinking about the face of our friends if we even thought of going back... I tried, time and time again, to think pleasantly of the regime's mission.

I looked for the pleasure in never feeling satisfied. I talked about it with Ruly. From young, they taught my siblings and I to leave something on the plate out of good manners. That leftover food was given to the dog, who also ate chicken bones, rice, croquetas, sweets, and chocolate bread. Ruly mentioned that a dog was luckier than we were. At what moment did we get into this, he asked without tone or interrogation, without any accentuation. I looked at him in such a way that I wouldn't dare to repeat now; in some way I despised his cowardliness, that which was none other than an effect of my own.

Two months in, after calls and messages of encouragement, a meeting was called to share our improvement. As if in the air you could breathe in the suspicion that someone broke their promise of being vegan, each one of us gave our testimony of how we felt. It was a wake: we spoke softly, almost in whispers, and we all looked at each other without a sense of trust. However, the group seemed to be following the right ideals; there was nobody brave enough to raise their voice against them. With feverish eyes, we elevated chants taken from our hands: We're all living beings! The planet has the right to be free! Even though Ruly seemed optimistic almost all evening, it seemed to me the group looked depleted in general and nobody wanted to accept it. It can't be that I was the only one who noticed the bags in the eyes of the faces of everyone else; I had the impression even that everyone's movements were slow, even if it was to get out of the seat or to share a specialized magazine with an article expressing interest for being vegan. We were different people. That was the night I looked in the bathroom mirror and I got scare of my reflection: my sunken eyes looked as if they wanted to scream at me for how stupid it was to worship this absurd, raised flag despite the evident decline. I felt like the end was near, even though I also saw clearly the impossibility of communicating it.

Some more days passed, maybe 10 or 20 or 100. If you're falling to pieces, it gets hard to tell time. Following the initial routine, I kept doing the grocery shopping while Ruly was in charge of buying organic supplements in a special shop that was on his way home from work. It was in the wine and liquor aisle where I decided to put back a bottle of red wine, suspecting that it had egg whites and yolks, tempting territory. I was about to put back the Merlot – that moment when the object stops belonging to your hand and gets reintegrated with its original space – with the intention of running back to the house to make one of our frugal meals when my eyes stopped on an insanely beautiful package of pork rinds. It was red to call the attention of hungry consumers and had a noble-faced pig and a little transparent window to admire the product from what it looked like on the inside. I gripped the bottle tightly, I put it in my lap as if it were a creature, and I hesitantly advanced towards Hell.

My steps, at that point, were uncertain. I sensed that it was a bad thing in my left ear, which obviously impeded a balance consistent with my height and my weight: the latter, in clear decline. I moved carefully, reproducing each step first in the mind. I must say that it was not hunger that made me fall, but a certain pulsation in my taste buds. The recognition of that salty and spicy taste obfuscated my sense of alliance. I went over, bottle in hand, until I was one step away from the infamous creature. I caressed my burden for a long time, in absolute contemplation with that temptation in a bag ready to go; for seconds, that protected me from greater sins, preserved the distance between desire and the fatal bite.

I couldn't do it anymore. I dropped the bottle, threw myself into the bag, trying to memorize its nutritional table as a mere exercise of entertainment: Calories, 282. Sodium, 989 milligrams. And the same with cholesterol, zero percent vitamins... at the end in large letters: 100% natural pig. I turned around; I saw the pig with his benevolent smile saying: "Take me. This is your chance." As if I were about to bite my lover's lips, I tore the bag with my teeth: the scent of processed pig penetrated my nose, giving the last stab to my integrity. I devoured a pork rind, and then two... in the end I came to the cash register with the bag completely empty. I was not going to commit a crime: the cashier finished scanning my groceries and asked me if she could throw the package in the trash.

I arrived home with my senses alert; the shrieks of the animal sacrificed for the ocasion resounded in my guts. Ruly wore a sweater even when we were in the middle of summer; he came over to give me a bird kiss, those kinds of kisses that enriched our contact since the night of evil. As we were cooking a bean tortilla, we alternated bland comments about the weather and the latest health news in a couple of electronic journals to which we had subscribed. In such a small kitchen, it was difficult for more than one person to get around. We were close, so close that I could feel his breath: I was terrified that he discovered my sin.

We ate in silence, I acted out any stupidity and slipped out of the room to sleep twenty minutes before returning to the office. In my sleep, I felt his body slipping into the bed. I heard him say: "Let the assassins pay for their sins." Upon awakening, Ruly was literally crucified on the bed. With his arms crossed and his gaze fixed on the ceiling, he said incoherent things. I kissed him on the forehead. I ran to the office.

On my way home at night, I went to a famous place where mothers talk while their children play by salivating on colorful balls. I ordered a beef burger combo with a vanilla milkshake. The tray looked beautiful with its cardboard containers and sachets of condiments. My observation was almost mystical: I wanted to be aware of what I was about to do.

I was going to betray Ruly. Again. And I was going to betray everyone. I eliminated the word from my thoughts, instead I chose the phrase: "It is wise ..."; then I linked it with a slogan that I remembered right at that decisive moment: "Listen to your body: it knows what it needs." The morsels of meat fell in my stomach like manna sent by God and the milkshake was rain in the desert of my soul and my convictions. I felt the benefits immediately.

I entered the house in a good mood, with a sharp spirit, ready to do something different that would shake the morass of recent times. Ruly baked rye muffins: he was very proud of the new recipe. He said he would share it, or risk that they would be better off the second time with our friends at the next meeting. While he was talking, I imagined the delicacy with which I would satisfy my fleshly desires the next day: maybe a hot dog or pork chops. I got excited just thinking about it. Ruly continued with his recipe. I changed the subject and proposed a movie. He did not answer me, although I'm sure he heard what I said; maybe he was torn between the difficult task of answering yes or no.

From some cavernous place of myself came the provocation: "We have become zombies. Look at you." He continued on his own, without flinching. I insisted. I was so restored that I looked for war, a little lawsuit, a flash to upset the desire. I wanted to antagonize him, to provoke a war-like reaction in him. I was seduced by the idea of stings in my conscience to appease the guilt of having betrayed him and, what's worse, to be enjoying at the same time that he exercised again and again my right to betray. I tried to draw his attention to the film, but his concentration was limited. He seemed to be as sleepy as ever. I asked him if his eyelids were heavy and he looked at me as if trying to recognize me: "Look how much you've changed. You did not ask those things before. "

Knowing that that could bother him, I dragged him his attention to the movie as we settled in front of the screen to watch *Only Lovers Left Alive:* two contemporary vampires overcome the ancestral habit of killing to eat and have loved each other for hundreds of years. He was so fragile that he let himself go without replying. Before he looked with anguish towards the kitchen. I said sarcastically: "The oven will warn us when they are ready." At the beginning of the movie, the protagonist's effort to get uncontaminated blood to survive was so badly presented. Ruly leaned his head on my shoulder to fall in a restless numbness. Several times I heard the effort with which he drew air. It was the first time I heard that high-pitched sound, a whistle that seemed to come from the wind but was emerging from his accelerated chest. I decided to leave the movie for later. He accepted that we better read in bed, as in the old days when we wanted to analyze words and make love between one dissertation and another. It was when the gestures, the courage for not succeeding in putting together a dignified prayer, much less defending a position.

The narrator of Chesterton speaks about how conceited it is trying to convince someone of something. "If I have never experienced certainty, I cannot say that anything is true." I like this point and jot it down with a pencil; instinctively I take his hand and feel the cold under the sheets while I raise the volume of my voice. His hand in mine is a piece of ice that begins to fall apart. He is so emaciated that he could see, if I proposed, how his cheekbones sink with each breath. Deep down he knows the incomprehensibility of his diatribe, but vanity prevents him from accepting it. With a grimace of an old man, he seems to struggle to imprison the words. Look at the ceiling with meticulousness, scrutinizing every corner, the cracks, an ancient mark, to look for answers Then, he tilts his face like a doll and looks at me with anguish: he cannot believe that we are now so different, if only a week ago we were dying at the same rhythm.

Suspicion in the haze of his eyes confronts me, pokes at me, cuts me into thin strips. He turns on his side, drops his hand on my stomach, and falls asleep almost immediately. With his movement, I feel that the bed is a burden with more weight on one side and that it is tilted in an impetuous sea. If we are shipwrecked, I will fall first into the water. I get distracted by those stupid things. In the back of his mind and everyone's, I know they're stuck on my mistake, while their sense of reality, "although cracked for a moment, remains intact." Seeing him helpless, I want to say that I have been saved behind his back. I cower, how can I confess the unspeakable?

Just as the cycle of destruction of traitors prescribes, in the morning I woke up with a twinge of guilt in my stomach. Ruly couldn't believe how it had occurred to us to sleep without dinner; just to remember my banquet from the previous afternoon, I went to another phase: mechanization. I spoke, while we were having fruit and rolls with a few grams of coconut oil for breakfast, about what a beautiful day it was. I mentalized an intimate party, the most special occasion of recent times. The table adorned with a red tablecloth: an idea perhaps arising from the image of a vampire, laying on the couch after having ingested his cup of blood. I said, almost without thinking: "See you at seven. I will take advantage of my lunch time to buy blueberries and nuts. "

The Epicurean stamp of a snack on that table lost me. For the first time in two months I thanked Ruly for his silence, with the devotion of a companion who knows what his partner is going through. I remembered the *barbecue* ribs that had exalted my senses in one of the old meetings with friends. It was easy to choose the accompaniments: when the universe is silent, sins become more creative. Fried rice with hard boiled eggs. If Ruly had been more knowing, he would have suspected the way my eyes shone. Someone once said to me: "If you are going to sin, sin well." I added some bacon to the garnish.

We said goodbye and everyone went on their pursuit of survival. My idea — and anyone who has been unfaithful will be able to understand me — was to be cautious. I planned to leave the office early using any excuse, buy what I needed, get home shortly before three o'clock, with enough time before Ruly arrived at six. My thought was a perfectly ordered room. First, I thought about putting some music, but

I rejected the idea. The intimacy was enough to accommodate a pleasure of that size.

After a fruitful shopping day, the elements jumped to my eyes for strange cosmic associations. I put together the preparations. In less than an hour, if my calculations do not fail, the atmosphere was conformed to the height of the best seduction story. I complemented the red tablecloth table with a wicker center in which I placed with infinite love: ribs, sauces and garnishes. True to what my mind had gestated, that was a model worthy of franchising. With the expectation fulfilled of a lover who sees the bed set and the subject of naked passion, the desire ignited my desire. It was the moment when I lost my sense of time.

I wandered, in a kind of dance, around the table to see it from different angles. I placed myself in the chair next to the window, where the lighted candles flickered. The pacholí essence spread quickly and melted with the aroma of the dishes. I reflected a little with my hands together before the spectacle of the flesh at its point, of a golden chestnut on the surface and with that divine center about to be discovered. As in the best stories, penetrating the meat with a knife and fork was just enough pleasure to be savored. I could not contain myself, but I was determined to live the experience in tantric style: wait, hold, stop before the final outburst.

While the delight of that perfect flesh opened before my eyes, I got rid of all negative thoughts; I was grateful for the beauty of the world, for the animals that came to light the hedonistic hearts of a world violated by so much bad news. I still remember how confident I felt at the first bite. I enjoyed it with Zen serenity, giving due respect to the moment. I appreciated, just before seeing the clock, the teachings of Chesterton, the grace of being "lit inside like a lamp" and of never letting ourselves be carried away by the fury of a raging river, by the insipid desire to guard a certainty. I could not stop anymore. I bit and sucked those bones until they were clean.

I didn't notice that Ruly arrived until I faced him standing at the other end of the table. He saw me as if I were an intruder, a rat that would have to be exterminated to stay alive. I did not realize that his pants were so big on him. His hands, like the bird's claws of Borges's nightmares, touched me barely, they said goodbye with a light touch of foam, of dead wings. He said many things: hundreds, thousands.

It was not such a solid relationship. Today I know that conversation is not enough. The threat of a decision breaks everything. I'm sure. I was since he opened his mouth and started with his babbling, that his ability to elaborate coherent ideas no longer existed. But I wonder: can a person be absolutely certain of something, anything?

The Animal

Getting his meal on time kept him strong and happy. Like all animals, he had his predilections. In the same way that herbivores do not eat meat and carnivores, herbs, he did not eat salt, sugar, pork, fat, or flours in excess. He only tolerated brown bread, slightly brown, almost tanned. White caused unbearable heartburn and, in extreme cases, gas; then the environment certainly became unbreathable, urging that you spray room spray in every corner of your space very much in spite of your allergy to sweet smells. We had to be careful with food preparation. Because of his sensitive smell, he was able to distinguish between a dish without salt to one loaded with spice or one that was overcooked. At exactly two o'clock in the afternoon the exact amount of proteins, vegetables, fresh fruits and carbohydrates was deposited on his table. He was fascinated by the icy lemon water. A jug was provided in the refrigerator every day.

He was an animal of insomniac nature. For this, he had to hire a television plan that included as much programming as possible for his dead hours. The animal liked that: it was very funny to have control in his hand and change the channel between dreams. A problem in his ear was the cause of the high volumes that caused continuous vibrations at unexpected times, when others slept. Frights couldn't wait and the cracks in the walls couldn't either. The animal screamed for days about the matter. As much as it was explained that the cracks were due to the high decibels that in turn produced vibrations, the animal remained firm in his courage and cursed the architect, the builder, the painter, the concierge of the building, the bad quality of materials to each one of us. He was an irascible animal, almost choleric. Of course, the above was only discussed among us so as not to irritate him. In addition, discretion avoided us during the bad time of certain attitudes, such as foaming at the mouth. Besides, he was spiteful and would never have forgiven us for that lack of respect: to speak badly about him behind his back.

He hated the heat. A powerful cooling device kept the space cold all the time. He was very happy to feel the moisture of his body disappear and in its place was a skin clean of drops and discomfort, like a porcelain doll. Sometimes he got angry at being alone and took a walk around the other rooms of the house; He liked to see us then, but at a safe distance. We should be able to intuit his presence so as not to face him directly. For this we became experts in the technique of parallel paths: a dexterity of self-control and motor skills based on sensory reflexes, an incredible ability to respond to their footsteps, however faint they might be, or even their wild strides, if that were the case.

Every morning the animal found along his newspaper fruits, juice, and an espresso coffee. Over time, some light yogurt and 100 percent natural hive honey were added to the menu. With stealth, we deposited the tray before he opened his eyes. It was not a pleasant sight. Up close they acquired a reddish hue, of uncovered winds. Around noon, they changed from red to brown and became much more bearable. With some imagination, they could be the eyes of gratitude.

The perfectly balanced breakfast was his fuel to start the day. When we returned to the dirty dishes, I thanked him in silence. It was the indication of having done the right thing because, like anyone of his species, he denounced the rupture of natural balance with grunts. He assured us that, to a greater or lesser extent, all the rest of us were stupid, even though it was difficult for him to understand such a lack in the universal plan. This happened, for example, when because of regrettable forgetfulness the honey was missing or the coffee was too light.

A couple of times a day he did gymnastic exercises suitable for an animal of his condition: stretching, trotting, and tripping. Twenty minutes were enough. This guaranteed an optimal cardiovascular state, so necessary for a healthy life. He checked his weight every day in order to verify the number of calories allowed for that day.

Someone must have told him that his voice was pleasant. He talked a lot in front of a mirror. If we had the bad luck to open the door when he was in full speech, he shouted at us for how clumsy and stupid we were so as not to sense that he was busy facing himself. In cases like this we retired because of how blind we were, for being intruders, with our tails between our legs.

He hated to distinguish the echo of our voices in the corners of the house. That's how we acquired experience in communicating with signs and codes of understanding that at least guaranteed us survival. The one I did listen to every day was the BBC in London. I used program after program, from politics to shows. I took notes in black notebooks in which I printed a seal that smelled like burnt wax. And the animal was tidy, an example of personal organization.

Despite the animal and also thanks to him, our life was relatively calm. We maintained an almost enviable state of comfort if we took good care of him; if not, we dealt with the consequences: a very easy to solve conditioning equation. Aware of our duty in life, we took care of him with the care and dedication that an animal of its kind deserved.

One night we were awakened by his grunts and we all rushed to help him. He shouted things that were unintelligible, curses, unconnected threats. With him in a bad mood, it was impossible for us to avoid long faces and a general discouragement flooded the house. You could touch the discouragement: a close depression united us in a kind of failed community. In the morning we left the tray in the room and we walked away trembling, protecting each other, like soldiers. No one dared to look for him. We were afraid that a terrible truth could be seen in that gale. We agreed to add carrots to the midday vegetables: they cheered up spirits and revitalized the desire to live. We also added beet because, as we read, it had been proven to reconstruct and worked as an antioxidant. For breakfast, we added toast with low-fat cheese, highly recommended to take care of the heart and joints. It was not that we missed his vitality, but common sense told us that we had to return it to its normal state to protect our lives. We were too young to die and we had a whole life ahead of us. We contemplated the possibility of heartburn, stomach pain, rheumatic fever, ulcers. We concluded that his health depended on us. How could we not take care of him if he was the animal of the house?

At noon, the tray was almost intact. He had consumed the coffee, but the egg and walnut marzipan were still there. He lay with his eyes closed, but he was not asleep. We knew the pauses in his breath perfectly. We left the tray as it was with some hope. Nothing. With dinner, the same. We had to withdraw the food of the day and divide the calories and carbohydrates between us because in that house nothing could be wasted. New inquiries arose: Did he lose his watch? Was the lack of coordination killing him? Andropause would be on his heels? Was he tired or bored? We checked the thermostat of the air conditioning system, the exact calories in his diet, the general conditions of his space, the softness of his sheets, and all of the things that crossed our minds as a potential warning signal. All our efforts caused only major outbursts.

At the first bite in the neck we agreed to stop treating him, with all the consequences we'd face. It seemed that he wanted to finish us with a slap. One day he found us in the kitchen closet, licking our wounds and drinking thyme and sage tea to calm the pains. He just said *I am the animal of the house!* We took it as a warning that he missed us: we were necessary. We concluded that, by not supporting his agenda, he felt more animal than ever in front of his victims. Our position gave us an advantage and we gave ourselves the luxury of ignoring it. He walked away dragging his slippers to his room. In retaliation, we would not take *Processor* or *The Informer* to him. Let him rot from ignorance and sadness! We had each other and he was alone. The pain made us strong. An invisible wall was built between us and the inconsiderate animal. We stopped giving him his food. We ate in silence and hardly exchanged a few words a day. Guilt began to take its toll: remorse won the game. We concluded that after all he was not an animal so different from the others and that the dark reasons for his behavior had to be understood. We planned a tour the next day in search of reconciliation. We would do it soon and we would recover the forgotten ritual, the breakfast pne. Surely opening his eyes would be pleased to see that we were willing to serve him again. How to explain? We needed the oppression and the slap, what some call the stick and the stuffed animal. We were not able to demand things of ourselves alone, to direct our lives for ourselves.

Even though animals sometimes smell bad, nobody noticed. We left the tray on the table. At the same time, trembling, holding hands, we fix our eyes on his. Immobile. The winds were calm.

The Prisoner

Sometimes I took you on a stroll around the park. As all women do when they're with someone of your size, I tried not to lose sight of you. As much as I complied with haircut appointments every month, you had a very funny fringe on your forehead, a curl you had to subdue with gel in the morning so you wouldn't get in trouble at school. You put your cap on backwards, you walked securely with your hands in your pockets and you made noises with your mouth: locomotive, wasp, and a whirlwind. One of my worries was to measure the instance in which we should stop our stroll; that's why I observed you, I measured every movement and I evaluated your reactions. You were someone who shouldn't reach the limit of your resistance. The doctor said that our condition was a more or less common one and that you'd grow out of it. Meanwhile, I made sure you didn't go crazy in games with others like you, especially when there were objects that could end up hurting you. Overall, those getaways always had a positive effect. It gave me the impression that we'd let some things go to come back to them later, the two of us, a little bit lighter in Ofelia's house, where we lived.

Ofelia looked at you with sympathy: to her, you seemed intelligent and above all very clever. She described you as clever, playful, talkative, aware; like those who do well in everything. The last thing she said very often when they asked for you on the street. She answered that you were mine and that things would go very well for you when you're older. She always answered that you were mine. She liked to emphasize that it was one thing for her to like you and quite another for you to be something of her own.

At breakfast, you'd get along so well that she even said that you were enchanting. You'd always say please, thank you,

you didn't make any noise with your mouth or with the silverware, and you didn't start eating until she gave us the signal to start. You had learned to eliminate excessive rhetoric in school commentaries. If you lost your composure and started to get excited, I would take you by the arm and you, so intelligent, understood my message and slowed down your words. At two we were amused to see you drowsy, not wanting to go to school, lazy; however, that could not last more than a few minutes, enough to wake you up well and recharge the energy needed for the day. In the afternoons, when she was good in a good mood, Ofelia played with you and together you'd build towers with colorful pieces that resembled LEGOs. You'd laugh a lot, say nonsensical thing, and salivate more just because you felt like it. After a while, you'd get tired and before you'd get restless, I would shake your hands, put on your shoes and put you in front of the TV. Meanwhile, Ofelia and I listened to music, each of us in our chair, and drank vodka with orange juice. At the right moment, I'd go to you to take you to bed. Sometimes you'd give her a kiss and she told you to behave well, as if you could do something bad while you slept.

One day you behaved very badly with Ofelia: you were making a tower and she was working on a highway. She put two pieces in your tower and it fell apart; you couldn't stand her messing with your tower and you threw a LEGO directly at her face, then another and another; I managed to stop you before the kicks and the punches, then you exploded in expletives that you heard from others at school. For Ofelia, the deed was unforgivable, a transcendental event, categorically definitive; for me, it was to be expected of someone who was growing up like you. Plus, mood swings were common in those your age, even more so in those who suffered from some kind of intolerance. As soon as I returned to Ofelia after putting you to bed and calming you down, she let me know she didn't want you around her ever again. My tactics were of no use, she remained unscathed. We could stay in her house forever as long I'd find a way to keep you hidden, without you two ever crossing paths again.

The basement, occupied by tools and old magazines, was not being used. I thought it could be an alternative place as the storm passed; that's what I thought at first, wanting to see something good happen after so much intransigence. With you pulling my skirt, I began to clean the place; I arranged your things: the toy drawer, the bed, clothes, and photographs. You just looked without asking. Despite the air conditioning, the room was still a dark place, poorly lit, cold at night and extremely hot during the day.

You knew what was going on perfectly. You were very smart for your age. The last day you were more attentive than normal. You stood by Ofelia's chair for a long time like a statue, waiting for redemption. Without speaking to you or turning to see you, Ofelia ordered me to remove you from her sight.

You threw a tantrum the first time I left you in your new room. I was afraid that you would become uncontrollable again and with that you'd spoil your last opportunity. You cried a lot the first few nights. It was evident that you were lonely; you missed your place with me. You cried and cried like when you were smaller and you took air to let out a squeal again. The neighbors complained about the noise that came from the house every night. They threatened to do something against you; *anything*, if we couldn't fix it. I understood; all neighbors complain about the same thing and nobody likes to have hours of sleep stolen from them. I started to come down to see you: I would hug you, I would sing to you for a while and when your eyes shut, I would hurry up and lie down silently next to Ofelia to confirm that, once again, everything was at peace. I fell asleep thinking about the neighbors: insensitive bastards who would surely be listening, willing to seek revenge.

Before Ofelia woke up, I heard the sound of your spoon against the plate while you ate breakfast, surely cereal. I imagined you sitting at the table, alone in that room, looking at the wall, without me and without anyone. I felt a bite in my stomach, but the house was Ofelia's and I could not oppose that. Later, I took you to school and tried to make up for it: I would check a hundred times that you were wrapped up well, that you weren't missing anything, and that you had some cookies on hand in case you got hungry. You, with your face pressed to the window, rode all the way with me without speaking. Coming back home, you'd cry when I served you at the little table in the room while Ofelia and I ate in the dining room.

One night I heard you and I went down the stairs quickly to see you. Curled on the ground, you grumbled something to yourself. The bed was wet and turned upside-down. I changed the sheets and tried to help you put on some dry so you could sleep in peace. You didn't allow it, instead, you clung to my legs when I wanted to leave. I had to lock the door behind me. You needed to understand that for the time being you would be okay there in the room.

The strolls stopped working. You did not want to play with others or walk with me. On the way back, I had to carry you to the little room, and with a lot of work, help you in the bathroom and prepare your things for the next day. When I finished, I hurried to lock the door. Ofelia, without saying a word to me, left the bed and went to her couch where she could no longer here your bangs on the door.

You lost weight quickly, so much so that you seemed much younger than you were. I fulfilled the respective functions with someone of your age: I took you to school in the morning, I picked you up after work, I took you to your room, then I ate with Ofelia. You no longer made noise or cried; your outbursts calmed down and you spent most of the time glued to the door, with your eyes fixed on your box of

LEGOs. I know because when I opened it you were always there: the glassy look, almost without blinking.

One day, on the way to school, you finally opened your mouth and told me you hated me. I understood, although it hurt, because you were mine and no woman to be told such things from someone who's hers. The following days you said it frequently and as you did it, color returned to your cheeks and, like in the old days, you made noises and salivation while laughing. I was happy to see you happy again. Ofelia told me that you were getting better and she even said that when you were big, things would go very well. You stayed in the room, but there was no need to lock it. Our communication was limited, I heard you say you hated me, but I did not care, just to see that little by little you recovered. I even accepted that kicking and biting were part of the process. The more violent you got with me, the better you looked. Maybe the doctor was wrong and your intolerance was not as bad as he said.

Once again, the three of us go for a walk. Ofelia says that you are very nice and that she's please by you being fun and funny. She gives you her hand to cross the street. I notice your reactions all the time. When you start to get difficult, I stroke your head and with that simple contact, you scream at me that you hate me with all your heart and do not stop until you recover and breathe normally. Then, like everyone of your age, you play, have fun, do something stupid. At some point you get tired as everyone does, and since I take care of you I get closer, I try to hug you and you pounce on me to bite me, to hurt me, to tell me how much you hate me.

Elba Juárez

It was a myth that I was determined to deny. *Elba Juárez is the only one who can help you*, they told me. By then I had gone through everything, from the longest and most expensive psychological therapy in history to a clean one with an egg and herb from the hands of a witch as famous as he was expensive. To a certain extent I insisted on balancing my internal forces. I allowed a woman to put bunched up newspaper around my feet, spray it with alcohol, and set it on fire to scare the evil spirits that inhabited me once and for all. Another event, perhaps the most shameful, was that of shrieking coal, burned alive: when it passed through my whole body, specifically the genitals, it reached unbearable decibels, to the point that I asked the bonesetter who took care of me to leave before I went crazier. She only agreed after charging seventy percent of the total cost of the treatment and that because the coal had not been consumed completely.

All you have left is Elba Juarez, they insisted, *Elba Juarez has pulled worse oxen from the ravine*, and so on, and so on. I ignored the recommendation as long as I could, until I called out for it on one of the stormiest nights of my existence, when I swore to my roommate that a cockroach was hanging around my sheets. I had seen it with the corner of my eye and I was sure that it had seen me too. *Cockroaches are blind*, she told me, *besides, there is nothing, look closely*. The rest of the night I searched unsuccessfully for the invader. The next morning, I showed my roommate the rash on the backs of my knees and feet, there was no doubt, the cockroach had walked *on me*, walking all over my arms and legs as it pleased, my stomach, its antennae had pecked my face and my ears. My friend ignored the evidence, sighed for a long time, and ranted to me about how upset she was to see the conditions I was in, the stress she felt, and how difficult it was to be with me. *Mistrust is another disease*, I told her when she slowly pronounced d-i-s-e-a-s-e, surely to overexaggerate my situation and become the martyr, a role that, by the way, suited her well with the figure of a dramatic protagonist who had crafted and polished herself for years. That righteous night I got tired of hurting people. Elba Juárez's time had come and I could no longer postpone it.

I got lost several times before arriving. The oldest and scruffiest building on the block was hidden in a strange horseshoe surrounded by skinny little wings. I thought that like all the previous consultations this one would start a half an hour later, so for the wait I put the poetry of Oscar Oliva in my backpack. In those days I used to cover the books with plastic, put my name in them and my contact information. I was in a panic that one day they wouldn't be returned to me and become doves without memory or direction.

From the beginning of the week I had been hoping that she would give me a prescription with a good dose of *Valium, Rivotril,* or *Clonazepam* and we would end quickly with the theater of understanding and clinical comprehension. The three hundred pesos that the consultation cost should include at least three to five refills, otherwise the investment of a full afternoon would not be profitable. Any of those angels was good enough for me, they tamed my beasts and made me a reasonable and almost happy being. I wanted to be in front of a pharmacy counter soon. That evening *Vertigo* was on television showing the scene of the protagonist trying to climb slowly to a footstool. Hitchcock's women at the bottom of the stairs had been interrupting my sleep a week before when they announced the transmission. I did and didn't want to see Madeleine again having coffee with the detective; the cliff's kiss gave me unforgettable excitement. Sometimes I felt like Madeleine and sometimes Judy, I put my hair in a bun and didn't dye it blonde because the smell of peroxide gave me coughing fits. Other than the film, as if that were not enough, that same night I had to consume fettuccine pasta whose packaging signaled a very close expiration date, its preparation would take me at least fifteen additional minutes plus what it would take me to bathe, undo and redo the bed to save me the risk of unwanted pests. I'd have the time if Elba Juárez saw me on time. But if she fell into the sin of unpunctuality like most of her colleagues, I would curse those who rang in me the bells of chimerical Elba Juarez.

I filled out a card with all my data, except for the questionnaire I left blank. The secretary was not interested in knowing if I was afraid of being alone or what kind of sensation the color red or ants provoked within me. As soon as I wrote my name, I discovered it by reading the questionnaire of another patient. I hate intrusions and especially bandits that steal information. I had to wait for her for a half an hour in the room surrounded by doors. Elba's room was twenty-seven and it was the only one painted with a kind of greenish patina. Despite the secretary's penetrating smell of the nail polish, I tried to read, *I climbed on the podium of my heart / it broke on Tuesday / Saturday is anticipated on Mondays / the dream rises from Lazarus' mouth.* Curiously, it was Tuesday, Tuesday, June twenty-six, and my red *Citizen* showed it was almost half past four in the afternoon when the hinges of the green door creaked and finally emerged, as if from a shower of stars, Elba Juarez herself.

She said my first name smiling, *Gabriela.* It was not a question but an affirmation, Gabriela. I felt uncovered, naked like Judy after she came out of the bathroom with a broken bun and Scottie's expectation of having gotten her to become Madeleine. I nodded awkwardly, stood up and threw some things and when I went to pick them up, they caused others to fall. I have decided to carry only the indispensable and I have not been able to free myself from the attachment to deodorant and oral spray, less to sweets in case anxiety attacks me. With the signal from Elba Juárez, I walked towards unknown territory.

She walked around the room. It seemed to me that she was dancing a type of slippery dance.

How are you? I did not expect such a direct question. A less elementary interrogation would have left me more satisfied. My own silence froze me. I didn't know what to do with her gaze. My most recent pains sprouted from my mouth: the headache, the backache, the forehead pain, the eye pain and, although there are those who say that bones do not hurt, the sternum.

We sat facing each other. She occupied her wicker chair with clamps; me, the violet sofa. The yellows, greens and reds of Monet's Japanese Bridge fell down her lap in an almost liquid spill from her waist to her ankle. She crossed one leg over the other, an espadrille stopped mid-calf showing yellow-painted nails and the biggest foot I've seen. Her hair exposed her earrings, two black circles: the swings of a magical creature.

I'm sure her foot greeted me by looking at it like the ticking of a cartoon alarm clock. The smell of myrrh penetrated my airways all at once, I made an effort not to cough. Another scent, sweet peppermint, seemed to come out of her hair, armpits, throat when she spoke, hoarseness in her voice, so delusional, so trickster.

She began with my obsessions. The third time I put my hands in my bag to make sure my car keys were there, she asked me, *why do you do it? I'm nervous*, I told her. One of her hands fell like a bird's feather on mine: It felt huge and solid, as if it were a warm blanket. I didn't want her to take it off, I didn't want to, but she slowly withdrew it, hooking her pinky at the end with one of my fingers. It was a sticky heat.

It took me several Tuesdays to understand that the stupidest way to waste Elba Juarez was to let time tick in silence. The question, *how are you?* It was a detonator. After a few visits I learned to immediately release the answer, in defense of precious time. Silence was a lead creature, devouring the minutes.

One Tuesday, before lounging in her chair, Elba Juarez stopped being so tall despite the heel of her red suede boots that stood out like clappers from her bell bottoms. In a fleeting approach she brushed her face with mine. That Tuesday, unlike her normal Tuesday, she got up several times and traveled the distance to her desk in deep thought. Today I think of the charm of that wrist's flexibility in trimming, folding and unfolding a paper body, as in the frieze of drunkenness. *I'm not hyperactive, it's just that my blood pools and I have to get it moving,* I thought it was unheard of for Elba Juárez to explain.

Sometimes I wake up with those red boots in mind. I was wearing them on the twenty-fourth of Tuesday when I opened the floodgates to my demons. Nothing, not even the famous ingredient of Clonazepam, the protector of memories, prevents my brain from reliving the details with unbearable precision: the skin, the elegance of the heels, the glass oracle in the buckles.

One afternoon she established a relationship between my inner conflicts and the way I sit, going forward she kept asking me to try different positions. She wanted to know in what position I got in touch with my feelings, a pending sore, a nook only removable under that special stimulus. Perhaps her goal was also to exercise an impulse on my pliable person, to play dolls. I learned to obey: I must say that docility is not one of my virtues, perhaps it is instead of imitation, duplicity, the second part. So, she adopted a posture and I reproduced it.

The first version with which she sent me to the dressing rooms was that of my ten-year-old self. She asked me to write a fragment, a task from Tuesday to Tuesday. I arrived with half of a page because I easily lose the linearity of writing. I titled it *Return*, in absurd literalness to my teenage notes. She celebrated a few lines *the gardens of bushy red, purple, lilac bougainvillea, the talking silence of the old tunnel, I sweated, smelling that ancient moisture, stepping on the same pests, those that so long ago jumped on my shoes, climbed up my legs.*

On another occasion she asked for an account of the events that took place from my birth to my first decade. I invented an emergence to life with special characteristics. Rather than speaking, I wanted to hear her, so I reduced my comments to the indispensable minimum, enough to unleash her response, her interference, her comment. I was too smart not to notice. She punished me with what could hurt me most: a theatrical indifference in which I did not exist and she wandered around the room as if she thought about something; She took her chin, looked out the window and pretended to check a note in his rainbow cover notebook until she gave the terrible verdict: *I'll see you Tuesday.*

A paragraph by Oscar Oliva reminded me of a song stanza, a piece of something I heard when I was nine, ten, or eleven. That parallelism made it difficult, it opened a new knot: not to perish in that memory was the chant. I managed to get some Tuesdays, struggling with the recollection that I never found but brought out other beasts of the past.

When I lost my *Citizen*, I also lost hope in synchronizing my time with Elba's clock; I'm sure she was five minutes ahead, five precious minutes in my favor, which means she owed me five minutes for twenty-four Tuesdays: one hundred and twenty drops of soul that will never be replenished. However, I like that the invisible thread of being her creditor matches us in some way, perhaps in the way that the living are still attached to the dead by that damn act of imagining: the downfall of sleepwalkers.

Come in Gabriela Mistral, she announced one afternoon when I had absolutely nothing to say. With her face pressed to her window with fabric curtains, she invented what to say, what new problem to bring to light, to make time out of lost time. My genealogy had me deeply bored. That happens with genealogies, they run out, they have a limited number of characters; just like stories, even the densest, one day they finish being told. I was thinking about how to make the most of that glorious day. I could throw away any day, but not a Tuesday. She approached me, to watch my confusion closely. An insect crashed into the window leaving a milky star-shaped footprint. The heat raged in the street. A parked car shot a spark at me that lost strength at some point. That shock was what brought me back to the reality of the countdown of my suicidal minutes. Elba was still next to me, standing at the window: a giant. With an unusual cry, I became miserable, needy. The Island of the three Mermaids of Wallace rested on her desk. Her peppermint armpits hugged me tenderly, it was as if my mother, my sister, my daughter, my dog, Hitchcock, Madeleine, Oscar Oliva, all hugged me together.

Elba was made of ivory and at the same time of cooked mud, perfidious to hit the sharp nerves and the most tender in crises of cries and desolation; that is, she was the one who provoked and cured them. I wanted to cry to be hugged, I would not otherwise be able to wrap myself in that cloth whose engravings told a story of animals, people, plants, all in a single universe and spirit.

On Monday nights I used to invent next day's thoughts. You had to study and prepare something that could move her. A pain in the sternum, for example, alone would not get you another minute. I managed to convey the same, but with more color; I wanted to reflect the exercise and the task. One memorial afternoon she stopped in her comments longer than the regulation, she gave me seven more minutes, seven joys especially for me, not caring that another patient was waiting for her.

The day we talked about names was the prelude to hell. *Elba means elf,* she told me, *Nordic elf. A spirit in the air dancing with a line from Gabriela Mistral,* said and recited, *without name, race or creed, naked of everything and herself. Gabriela, Gabriela, what am I going to do with you?* The question trembled on its own. I said that my name came from the archangel Gabriel, who was in charge of announcing to Mary that she was going to be the mother of Jesus. *You're protected by God, you see, someone like that doesn't need therapies,* she said. Her words were lead. In a single blow she announced that she was leaving the city, the details do not matter. Elba Juarez was leaving, as if nothing, taking that and every Tuesday, my ephemeral happiness. That afternoon she drank an almost colorless tea, played a few moments with the infusion, until she left the spoon and asked me, *how do you feel?* I wanted to tell her why the hell did she care about how I felt, screaming at her that I had considered her incapable of abandoning her dead, just like that… but when I started crying I couldn't contain myself anymore and she had to come over to tell me things, to take my hand, to cover the pain of losing her.

I hated the substitute even before I met her, for being an outrage, an invader, a stepmother. They told me later that she was the perfect substitute, with the addition that punctuality was one of her virtues. I did not believe it, nobody can be better than Elba Juarez, thinking about it even broke my longing, fragmented my memory of her to such an extent that I made an appointment and went right on time, ready to unravel the damage. At four o'clock the door opened, a witch appeared in the doorway and approached me, greeted me with a kiss on the cheek and invited me to come in. I hated the dishonesty of her courtesy, the perfect coordination between the color of her blouse and her shoes ... after an unbearable forty-minute session that seemed like a thousand, I paid for a prescription and left Elba Juárez's office forever.

Perishables

You are rotting. I said it twice. First, before the rusty skin of an orange, then in front of the sheen of a mango's surface. In it, the shell was as hard as its contents; I was sure that not a drop would come out of that dry body no matter how much someone tried to squeeze it to the last drop. The mango, on the other hand, fooled me first with its bright appearance and made me believe that all colors melted into it. Illusory, I cupped my hands around that turgid body waiting for a sign of good tone, of certain firmness that would open the way for me to satiate my tooth. But nothing. It softened in a matter of seconds. That is worse. When the image says one thing and the interior another, one suffers alone. When you are on a diet, it is common to fall into the trap of appearances. Bodies acquire wrong dimensions with respect to what they really are. Instead, the truth crashes into itself; that one is very crude and infamous, as it is. Before throwing it into the trash can, I squeezed the mango without looking. Without regrets, I did the same thing that could bring me delicious sections. I told one and then the other. You are rotting.

I am able to produce catastrophic thoughts; sometimes I do it as a strategy not to think about worse things. I may seem like a pushover, but my own words scared me. You are rotting. The three words thundered in my mind with the force of shrapnel, as if they had been pronounced by a murderer who stalked every one of my movements from his hiding place. I even had the urge to get under the table to be safe from the deadly fragments. The resonance of that sentence surprised me to the point of panic. To calm down, I turned to the window and tried to admire the afternoon, but that was not possible. My reflection in the glass confronted me and put me to the test: to see if I dared to say it in its face. Looking into my eyes,

I pronounced them slowly, in the same way that food should be chewed to achieve optimal digestion according to my nutritionist. You are rotting.

I was startled by the sound of my wide's slippers, much like the drag of a mollusk, barely noticeable to the ears of human beings. She surprised me by muttering and, as usual, faithfully took advantage of the circumstance. Whenever life gives you that gift, you know how to get the most out of it. She got into where she was going – as always, only thinking of herself – put a mixed meat wheel (half pork, half beef) in enough oil, drenched the bread with mayonnaise and *light* mustard and finally put the meat in the center. While all this was happening, she pronounced the same curse as always. Her laugh went from the least to the most decibels. She mocked me until she was fed up. I didn't listen, since I finally know by heart what comes out of that cavernous mouth in these cases, I watched her do it, obsessed by her mastery: while she was carelessly having dinner, I could not find one healthy fruit. Her position of obvious superiority was a matter that paved the way for satisfying her gluttony from the beginning, a sin that she has committed with pleasure since I met her. She always comes at the worst time, when I am in one of my intimate debates. She had discovered me and that made me explode. The madman of the house doing his own thing and causing the grotesque hilarity of his wife. Who tells me to believe in the privacy that is entitled to every human being. Exhibiting myself like this, loudly, crying out for the health of the sick, demanding life where there is none. Caught at fault, I felt unprotected. I began to feel chills on my arms. Then I did want to hide, where her insults could not reach me. All this put me against the wall, ready for the final projectile that would kill me once and for all. Before leaving the kitchen, with the banquet in her hands, she looked at me with a condescending false attitude, then gave an exclamation to the wind, hands raised as if imploring help from beyond. Impossible to reproduce it. I resist being complicit in the proliferation of profanity. Nothing new. She had said what she always says, but this time her words were loaded with a deadly edge that pierced my soul, leaving me with the strength of a rag, with no will in my legs or arms, with my tongue out. A world of debris collapsed on my back.

It all starts with what you put in your mouth. It is the nutritionist's favorite saying. Fruits and vegetables work miracles for a person. Motivated perhaps by that truth, my eagerness to get colorful food in good condition was restored when I could. All the houses in the universe have fruits inside, I thought about the purpose of my thoughts. What was I going to tell her? I'm sorry, Miss Doctor. I could not follow the suggested diet because all the fruits of my house were about to die. I hope you understand me. I am not able to eat dying organisms. The pretext was too stupid! And if I also told her about the conversation my wife laughed at about a bloodless mango and a pathetic orange, she'd feel a compassion that would be hard to resist. I am not willing to let them mock me. I promise it to myself again. Neither now nor will I never give in to the impulses to express myself without thinking about the consequences. Women often take the smallest opportunity to enjoy the mistakes of others.

The refrigerator is a good place to preserve fruits. I contemplated, with some pity, the worn appearance of four strawberries that had been abandoned on a plate, without a lid, without a protective film, probably under the false belief that the cold prolongs life. What kind of evil. I hated who had everything to do with this and that seconds before had dared to say my name in a repulsive way: now I was the one who condemned his indecent action, the stupidity of always doing things wrong, the rotten breath of the woman who thinks she knows everything. In some corner of the house she was devouring her hamburger. Historical data indicated that the most likely spaces were the living room or the bedroom, both equipped with a television and enough cushions so she could settle without issue. One bite for the gringa series, another for the hamburger, a look at the stupid plot of lovers, another to the hamburger. I placed all my resentment on her, and slid the plate with the strawberries to the upper tray of the domestic morgue. You are rotting. I said it in a tone of redemption, almost in a murmur, with dissolved hope as if I passed it through water. I stayed in the center of the kitchen, paralyzed, unable to take a step. I had the dreadful certainty that radioactive mines were more likely to be found in my house than something healthy to be digested by the natural mechanism of a hungry body. At the saddest point of my reflections, she came back. In flip flops, with the empty plate in hand, the satisfaction in her face of having swallowed even the last crumb of bread and the last gram of meat that was on the face of the earth.

I have heard that certain types of terrestrial mollusks feed on decomposing matter. People usually talk about these things in the rainy season. Mud and wet shoes cause mixed feelings. Not content with how aberrant her attitude was, my wife returned for more. She caught me in immobility, which is equally lethal as when she does it at the crucial point of my speeches. She returned to attack because that is what she's made for. In the blades that had become her hands I distinguished her intentions to throw me in the storage room, where even the dog could not find me. She spoke and spoke, knowing the negative power that her speech exerts on my mood. And she said and said, invented and reinvented worlds parallel to her and me in the center of that space. Everything that occurred to her broke out from that viperous tongue. That the diet made me sicker than usual. That I was not only hallucinating, but that I was a flimsy piece of trash made by my mother. At the mere mention of the one that gave me my life my blood boiled, it boiled for a few seconds in which I felt a bull fighting, able to attack the enemy with the cruelty of revenge in its horns, in the long and bristly tail. But I am nothing more than a lazy nobody, precisely as my mother said. I lost my feeling of grandeur, I came back to being warm, and then I finally reached my normal temperature. Then she seized my body, so in need of love, fruits and vegetables, an extreme weakness that incapacitated me to respond with the dignity of a good man. I reduced myself to nothing. I just absorbed the flood. To navigate the danger.

Everything that goes in must come out. My wife left the kitchen nimbly, with a happy stomach, her panties well placed, without the dignity to look at the holocaust that her words had caused. The nutrition expert was right. We are all one with nature. The orange, mango and crazy meat were about to perish at the same time in the same saucepan. The universal fried food of misery. Maybe I'm predestined to die with company. There's always comfort for the damned.

I have developed some expertise in making her insults disappear. Over time I have been refining an evasion technique, although its typical for men to lose their rhythm. I get distracted, I forget what I learned. That night, already in bed, I made a huge effort so as not to be riddled again. It was mere survival instinct that made me hug her from behind, like the old days. Her flannel pajamas gave off a slightly edible, certainly spicy aroma, as if she had washed it with a spiced ginger detergent. In need of company in the absence of food recommended by the doctor, I crushed my nose and prepared to sleep in those warm arms of cotton and fluff. But the injustice was greater than any possibility of approach. The bed creaked when she violently broke free of me. She was offended, even if it is hard to believe. Her rejection penetrated me to the bone.

When I was finally blessed by sleep, a grumble in my abdominal emptiness reminded me of the five red fruits written in the specialist's recipe. I did what I could not to wake her up, but there is no touch of a fly that she doesn't perceive. It buzzed just like one. How the fuck, she said in a lethargic voice, impregnated with Valium. Dragging sleep around the house leaves nothing good. The kitchen was a swamp. I thought about plums, cherries, something that would take away that desire to get into french fries and Coca Cola. I settled for a handful of dried blueberries. The expiration date was horrifying, but it was minor compared to that hungry mouth in my stomach. I cradled the bag in my lap for a good while. There I stayed, sitting in the flower chair, chewing like a pig, concentrating on my extra kilos so I wouldn't think of other sorrows. No one saw me, only the black tongues of the night that passed through the slits of the window. For seconds or years, I did nothing more than introduce those grieved fruits into my mouth. I slowly chewed each bite; I liked to feel them perish against my teeth.

When I entered the room, her snoring was consistent. Spirited. Needless to say, I slipped into bed in silence, but no one can succeed against the fury of the winds. What do you smell like? That breath in my ear, that pasty voice, slapped my sleepy soul. In absolute silence, as if her question desecrated a grave, I made myself safe between the sheets and prepared to dream about the nutritionist sitting elegantly in the flowered armchair with her legs crossed and her red hot toenails, she looked forward to approaching me, to try a little, to bite me. I dedicated myself to curling my monk-like body before her eyes while she ate a peach she craved. What are you dreaming about? Pulled with absolute abruptness from paradise to the mass grave, I wanted to go for a walk in the streets in search of a kilo of apples, to knock on the doors of the neighbors under any pretext, to get the feet of that cooking pot. After annihilating my fantasies with pleasure, she used her old tactic and pretended to be asleep, facing the ceiling, with the cowardice of the one who throws the stone and hides their hand. The atmosphere soured to the rhythm of her breathing, while I watched with morbidity her nose's movements, subtle, active, and subtle again regularly. Her trembling eyelids were given away by her wakefulness, swollen and throbbing, no matter how much she made the effort to be absent. Knowing she was awake made me want to repeat it. To say it again. Of gloating under the influence of those three words. I faced her face, which immediately reminded me of popular rumors regarding animals that move by brushing their body against the ground and at the same time led me to a very poetic resolution: to the ephemeral beauty, when the beating wings of a fly had its seconds counted. I approached as much as I could, with the stealth of those who do not seek to fall into the abyss, but only glimpse into the void by the edge. I am confident, but not so much. Bringing my face to hers was a risky action. My forehead was millimeters from hers. My eyes on her eyes, on her cheeks. I knew I was transgressing domestic laws. I gave her my breath. Misery would be refocused on her, before she could let go one of her insults again. I peered into the endless tunnel of her ear and spoke first, even when I would be the last one to do so. We are rotting, I said. I did not wait for her response. The sheets began to provoke an itching sensation impossible to get rid of with simple ointments and ointments. A fly came out of the woodwork and stuck its disgusting legs onto my forehead. It wandered around her with the ease of being on a path of flowers and shit. I left the bed in despair, intending to escape as soon as possible from the fire. I tried to get the doctor out of my mind, but I seemed to have her sewn to my body. With everything and that weight on my back, I joyfully opened the only Coca Cola available and served it in ice in a glass. I tore, almost with lust, the metallic bag of the fries, sprinkled one by one with chili pepper and seasoned with a pinch of salt. The new version of homemade joy.

Boats

Going to the movies every Sunday is a habit for me. I do it in the evenings, preferably, although midday functions offer the same showings and the additional benefit of being pretty empty. When my brothers and I were children, my mother always chose matinée and we almost always stayed twice as long since it was permitted. We played, already in our second round, "guess the scenes that followed." We'd guess dialogues and even how the actors would dress. Later, when my brothers no longer went, the game was over, and mom continued taking advantage of the double film; then I got extremely bored. She knew it, but something that I never understood made her take advantage of the opportunity to the fullest, unable to ignore her right to stay as long as she wanted. Someone told me later that you could go to another room and see another movie or that different films were going on in the same room; in my case it was never like that. Maybe that's why, because of my experience as a kid, that I rarely go to a matinée, as happened that June morning.

I woke up with no intention of facing my pending domestic tasks. I work all week, from nine in the morning to seven in the afternoon, and lately I get the impression that Saturdays and Sundays have fewer hours than the other days: they're just not enough. I woke up, had a couple of fried eggs with some ketchup from a day before, orange juice, and two cups of dark coffee. I cleaned the kitchen and went to bed again. The day before, Saturday, I had taken care of doing the week's grocery shopping. So, I could have very well stayed there all morning. I started reading the newspaper and I fell asleep again.

A world of water, like Felisberto Hernández's flooded house, covered my light sleep. Water everywhere: from the gaps in the wood of the doors, leaks in the roof and something as strange as if the walls were huge pieces of human skin from whose pores sprouted drops and drops and drops. I woke up with an uncomfortable feeling, covered in sweat, uneasy. I thought about catastrophic things, as if something very bad was going to happen that day. I needed to leave the house, so I decided to take a shower with cold water to wake up completely, I put on some lipstick, and went to the movies without even seeing the list of showings.

When I was arriving, the clouds were slightly darkened. Just in case, I parked as close as I could, a few meters from the place where I didn't need to put coins in the parking meter since it was a holiday. I did not realize then how inadequate my sandals were for weather like that kind; Leather straps are usually ruined by water. There was a row of about fifteen people at the entrance. When I took the last place, I'd be number twenty. Some drops began to fall, then a light drizzle, fine but consistent. Some took out their umbrellas. I reprimanded myself for not being prepared. A big-bodied man pulled up the collar of his jacket and adjusted his hat. There were those who looked at the clock, maybe to check how many minutes they would have to wait outside, or if the weather forecast predicted rain.

Mexican cinema is a place helped by a persevering public. The films that are shown are more artistic than commercial. I like that. While shopping mall cinemas are full all the time, the old cinema hosts a maximum of thirty or forty people in each show. Oddly enough, no one loses the opportunity to occupy a seat, as if everything was perfectly planned and had previously checked the room's capacity and number of spectators.

That afternoon the place looked less crowded, but for me it was fine. Although those of us who go to the movies are always the same, we do not know each other. Nobody wants to pretend. That is also good for me. On the other hand, the public is made up of older people; canes, walkers, cushions, almost all of them use bifocal lenses, listening devices, or both. I was sure I had seen the couple in front of me before: his wife was wearing glasses and a necklace which had a candy-colored pillbox hanging from it. Don Joaquin wore a badge on his shirt, fastened with a metal lock that was used to fasten cloth diapers; on the badge you could see other data written besides his name, as well as a photograph of him, visibly younger. He wore dark, huge glasses around his neck on a thin string. Notorious was the presence of hearing aids, as he struggled with a control in his shirt pocket to regulate the volume.

It was the only thing he knew about them: things like that can be observed while one lines up, especially if the line is slow, like what happens in Mexican cinema. As soon as the ticket taker took his place at the front door, the wife urged Don Joaquin with a push on his hip to move forward. The ticket taker, perched on a high seat, picked up the yellow cards, checked them as if someone would dare falsify them, and returned them after splitting them in two with a frantic movement.

As spectators we have already generated a tradition, film workers have worked there for many years. In the box office is a bad-tempered woman who wears the same straw-colored dress every Sunday. When entering the lobby, we continue in the row: that's when the ticket taker performs his second function and manages the flow of everyone to the room, in perfect order.

I like to look at the posters of the recently shown films, to see which ones I missed. This, without knowing the reason, makes me feel a little guilty, as if I were committed to seeing them all, without missing one. I was pleased to know that the movie on that Sunday was Portuguese, a film based on the novel by Camilo Castelo Branco, *Mysteries in Lisbon*. I could compare it to the novel; although I was not so sure of remembering the content at face value, I have always had the idea that films activate memory sensors if it has already gone through history on paper. One of the posters showed a good photograph and a hundred and ninety minutes of intrigue, false identities, romance, and violence.

I left the line and asked his wife to please save my spot. She nodded as she looked towards the door of the room, still closed. I interpreted her gesture and quickly bought some chocolates and an apple drink. After so many years of doing exactly the same thing, the shop assistant had developed an efficient technique to cut the fruit, place it in transparent plastic cups, and add a bag of chili and a slice of lemon. A systematic method that rendered identical portions. When she finished filling a glass of mango slices, she gave me my purchase, took my coins and went on with her work.

I reached my place in the line just in time. Don Joaquin grumbled when his cane got stuck in the carpet; his wife helped him to pull it out and commented something about the decrepitude of the cinema, how old it all was, that was no longer useful. He urged Don Joaquin to move again so he would not lose his way. Once I was in the room, I lost sight of them.

In the intermission, the sound of the rain was evident. I don't know what others could have thought, but I regretted not bringing proper shoes and once again I reprimanded myself for not carrying an umbrella just in case. People became uneasy. They looked towards the ceiling as if with that they could measure the density of the storm. I saw the same old heads, without identifying a single one. Some covered their ears; the man next to me put his face between his legs until the transmission of the film recommenced. The rumble was getting unbearable.

The rest of the movie played out in a very rough way. Shortly before the identity of the main character was revealed, the electricity went out and everything was left in the deepest darkness. The noise of the rain invaded everything, so much that it silenced the complaints, the anger, the screams of frustration. The absolute silence in the room contrasted with the raging racket of the water outside. For a moment I thought that when we left, we would find desolate territory, as if the city had been devastated by a war or an earthquake. Suddenly, the clerk and the ticket taker entered with mops and buckets. The water had begun to seep into the room. Everyone stood and moved. That was when I saw Don Joaquin and his wife. As if it were a replica of what I had observed in the line, she urged him to get out, very close to him, body to body. Don Joaquin may have grimaced because of the hearing device that he took out, looked at, and put away, because of the way he was being rushed out or because the end of the film had been left unfinished. The carpets were completely wet. The viewing room was emptied in a few minutes.

It had stopped raining. Surely in order to prevent water from entering every part of the cinema, the glass door had closed almost entirely, which failed to stop the pounding of the water. It was difficult to measure the magnitude of the flood in the street: it probably reached five feet in height. Like before, everyone's eyes were glued to what was happening outside: that impossible universe, unattainable. The ticket taker and the clerk ran from the room to the area where all of us were, filling and emptying buckets, giving impossible explanations. The fact was that there was nothing we could do.

Don Joaquin and his wife stood at a safe distance from everyone, as if they were about to raise their voices and give a community speech. Since everyone was in pairs, I only let myself decipher the conversations. Allusions were made to climate change in recent times, to the fact that in the city such a phenomenon is rarely seen, the spectacle that we would be giving after a glass huddled around, with faces of being victims of a kidnapping. Truth is, nobody could see us. The street was deserted and water covered the entire landscape.

Don Joaquin, who only looked with some sorrow at what was happening, suddenly became worried. He leaned against the wall, lifted a leg, took off a shoe; he was about to do the same with the other, when his wife reprimanded him:

- What are you doing, for God's sake. You will get sick if your socks get wet.

He showed no reaction to her words. Without shoes, he crouched calmly with the apparent intention of folding his pantlegs to prevent water from reaching him. At a distance it seemed this was a prudent and responsible action, however, his intentions were not so clear. The lady retorted again:

- No, no, no. Stop that, please, what are you doing? Do not even think about it. No, you're not going to stay like that. Put your shoes on. Enough, enough, Joaquin, understand.

Don Joaquin stared at her for a few seconds with a pleading look. He looked like a child asking permission, waiting for approval to roll up his pants. A boy with a tremendous desire to put his feet in the water. She patted him on the thighs and tried to force him to lift his foot to put a shoe on him, while saying:

- You already got wet. Your socks are wet, Joaquín. Now what are we going to do? You're going to get sick, you're going to get sick. I told you, but you never understand. I get tired of telling you things and you never understand.

The clerk and the ticket taker had opened the glass door a little; In vain, they swept the water out with brooms, then mopped and ending up doing it again. There was so much water in the streets that it entered through the free space between the floor and the edge of the doors. At last they gave up such a useless task and settled behind the counter of the cafeteria, like two soldiers. Very little merchandise was left in sight: a packet of chocolates, some tubes of mint pills and two or three glasses of fruit. The small refrigerator was unplugged, I guess to avoid power outages when the electricity came back on.

Don Joaquin, visibly affected, very nervous, with his shoes in his hand, walked with clumsy steps towards the high chair of the ticket taker, took a roll of programs and stayed there, looking at the street, ecstatic. His wife, pulling his sweater, did not stop insisting on how terrible it was that he walked around without shoes, as if nothing:

- If you had a little conscience you would not do this. Who do you think will take care of you start coughing and get a fever? Let's see what you do when you can't stand up anymore. You're crazy, Joaquín, totally.

As she walked with Don Joaquin, I peered between their heads, as if I was seeking some approval for her actions. I can assure you that we were all focused on him, more than what she was trying to do to stop him. He went to the counter of the cafeteria, where the ticket taker and the clerk observed the stillness of the water in the street, whose level did not diminish a millimeter. For the first time he opened his mouth and said, with a cascaded but audible voice:

- I don't want to, I don't want to, I don't want to.

His wife pulled him by the sweater in despair and told him:

- I'm angry, Joaquín. Don't you see how silly you're being? How ashamed I am of you?

Don Joaquin put the programs on the counter glass; before the indifferent look of the ticket taker and the clerk, he replied:

- I don't want to, I don't want to, I don't want to.

He did not say anything else. He simply extended one of the brochures on the glass with his hands, folded it into two parts, then four, folded the corners until, very proudly, he got a perfect paper boat that how showed everyone, lifting it high so we could see it. Some exclamations came from the small but consistent crowd that we were. I was very close, so I could see it precisely: it really was very beautiful. I wanted to touch it, to run my fingers on its sail, to do what Don Joaquin did next. He looked down, perhaps to check how much he had managed to roll up his pants even with the insistence of his wife. He delicately took his little boat, walked towards the doors of the street, two palms barely open. He squatted down as if he were twelve years old and left the boat in the calm, undisturbed waters of the street. He straightened his body slowly and stared for a few seconds, and when he was sure that the boat was strong enough to withstand the force of the water, he stood up. Applause burst from here and there, alive and boisterous they came from the compressed mass in the room. His wife retreated into a corner and did not speak again.

Don Joaquin returned to the counter, repeated the operation and made another ship, and another. We all wanted one. There came a time when several of them floated in the sea, very erect, as if they were made of wood or metal. Fascinated, we watch them wave in the docile waters behind the glass, until seeing them disappear forever.

Forty-seven pesos

Lina wears her name on a square piece of cardboard attached with a golden pin to the white collar of her dress. The bus left at night and she thinks it has been hours since her sister said goodbye to her at the bus stop, but not even one hour has passed. She realizes when she hears that someone says it's almost eight. Her sandals bother her. The heat of the land swells her feet to the point of breaking the straps. She doesn't want these to be broken too. She takes them off and places one foot on her calf, then the other. She feels the scab on her soles rise and fall.

The passenger on the left snores and drool drips down his open mouth. Lina turns to her right, sticks her head on the glass and looks out the black window. Nothing can be distinguished. Dizziness forces her to close her eyes. When she wakes the bus is stopped. There are few seats occupied.

Yeya lent her forty-seven pesos that she keeps inside a little bag attached to the belt of her dress. She nagged her with orders on the way to the city center: don't buy anything in the stops, be careful when getting off the bus, don't lose the paper with the address, don't be stupid and leave your place because someone else could get it, don't cover your nametag with your sweater so they can't see it, city men are bastards and not like those of small towns, *that this, that that, I'll let you know what to do, do not be afraid, pray, say this, don't say that, speak, be quiet ...*

Yeya was the clever one since she had already worked in the city. She knew how to read and crunch numbers, she returned to town with good money and after a few months she would go back. No way to ignore her efforts if the last time she even able to build two rooms of the house. Now it was Lina's turn.

She is thirsty, but Yeya *said… dry your lips with the tip of your tongue.* It is better to not drink water, then she would need to urinate and then what she was going to do? She feels the wheels tap on her hip, her black hair sticks to the window again and she goes back to sleep. When she opens her eyes, it is daylight. She touches the sack and it moves. Her neck hurts and her legs are numb, but she doesn't feel like moving and remains still. She lifts her backpack from the floor and hugs it, then puts on her sandals.

The man right next to her is reading. Lina looks out the corner of her eyes at all those black symbols, then observes the look of the man who follows the lines from one side to the other, sees how he gathers his two fingertips to turn the page and envies Yeya's novels, *damn* Yeya. Only she could read. She had completed the same two years of primary school that Lina did, but Yeya was able to write her boyfriend a *corrido* in white papers that she then sealed with a red kiss and a pierced heart.

Like all the girls in town, Lina worked at the tortillería. She got the bills mixed up and they wouldn't get paid at closing time, so the owner decided to put her where his business was not at risk. He taught her to weigh kilos and half kilos in square pieces of paper and close the corners in the form of butterflies.

Yeya made fun of Lina by saying she was not born to read or write. And it was true. Lina knew it. Not everyone was given the same things, but at least she dared to work in the city before the age of fourteen *ah, my Lina, now it's up to you*, her father said almost without looking at her. Her mother passed the cross along her face and put her hands around the little bag that held Yeya's pesos. From there, they walked together to the city, Lina listening to her sister's nagging. Lina could only hear her, her eyes glued to the ground that raised her black and blue strapped sandals. Her nerves made her sick to her stomach.

She feels that something hard itches an eye. She takes out the eye booger with her nail, looks at the yellow pebble and removes it with her teeth. She chews a little before swallowing it. They have no flavor yet she likes to eat them. Yeya always calls her pig. She has tried to spit them out, but now when she has them in her mouth she can't resist.

During the day the bus seems to move slower. They told her that she was going to arrive very early, that Yeya's ex-boss's friend would be waiting for her. She stretches her legs. She knows the look of the lady very well. She's been repeating it so that she does not forget: white, with brown spots on his face, freckles, they were called freckles. The man was surely going to accompany her, also white with an uneven, blondish moustache. Hairless. Bald and shiny.

Finally, the wheels stop. She can't stand the urge to urinate anymore. She's been crossing her legs for a long time and is afraid she may pee in her pants. She gets up almost at the same time as the man with the book and gets behind him, joining the row that accumulates in the center aisle. The man says it smells bad and covers his nose with one hand, he also complains about the pushing. She barely moves. The people near the front seats want to get in and Lina urges to get off to find the bathroom. She thinks that she would be ashamed to say *good morning, I am peeing myself for the love of God*. No, she will ask for a bathroom.

Lina almost runs to the sign of a blue woman on a white door. She leaves with her face washed, her backpack on her shoulders and her hair in a ponytail. She follows the few people who still travel to the exit of the platform. She checks her nametag and the little bag, the little bag and her nametag.

She stands still and looks everywhere. She sees so many people together that she gets scared. She nervously caresses the black letters of her name on the makeshift nametag that she still has on her chest. Yeya wrote it, *damn* Yeya. She had become accustomed to assuming the dialogues of Yeya's illustrated novels, and to return them to their place under the mattress, on the run, before the sister accused her of gossiping.

A lady like the one she has in mind approaches, she says *it must be you* and she answers *yes*, shows her the nametag, repeats her name twice, obeys and follows her. Lina compares the image in her mind with that of the shiny, bald man and deduces that it is the woman's husband. The girl is about ten years old. She looks questioningly at her parents and then at Lina. She drinks loudly from a can of soda while examining Lina's face, her damp black hair, the white collar of the dress... She scrunches her nose. Lina's mouth waters. The woman takes the girl's hand and says *let's go*. Lina follows them. Before she realizes it, she is already in the back seat of a car and with her backpack lying on her legs. She feels her bitter tongue and dry lips. The girl's questions make her nervous. She laughs with each of Lina's responses.

When she arrives at their house, she asks for water and tells the woman about the fear she has when getting off the bus, and that she has a little sister the size of the girl. With more confidence, she begins to chat tells her about the floods that destroyed almost all the houses in her town. The woman indicates where the drawer for her clothes, towel, soap, toothpaste and a brush are. She points to the shower and orders her to bathe. Already alone in the room, Lina takes another dress from her backpack, two pale blue panties, some chewing gum and a fine-toothed comb. Her nametag and the little bag came off. She leaves them in the backpack at the corner of the bed. In a hurry, she does the same with her dress and bra, still looking at the pleated curtain that covers the door. She hops in the bathroom.

The woman informs her at what time the beds are made, the days that the garbage gets picked up, how the man likes his coffee and the girl's breakfast. Lina doesn't understand much, she figures that city people talk too fast and say many things together.

The girl walks close to her mother, snooping Lina's scrawny and shrunken humanity; she notices the white palms of her hands, long straight hair caught with a clothespin, and the nervous giggle on her thin lips.

When Yeya's voice reappears at night, she remembers the day she said, *if you are ordered to do many things, don't be dazed, do one thing at a time, don't screw this up*, from the coffee with three sugars for the man to the dinner plates set up on the drying rack, with the washed spoons still dripping droplets, *the first time you get lazy they'll send you back*. The soles of her feet pulsate, she feels half out of it, and her eyelids are heavy with sleepiness. Every night she prays with her brown hands together, as they taught her, and she wakes up the next day with the Christian figure on her chest, then she places it on the nightstand with open arms and smooths the sheets before hearing the first *Liiiiiina* that wakes her up completely.

The days pass quickly and Lina learns the routine: Monday and Wednesday, wash the windows of all the bedrooms; Friday, clean the kitchen thoroughly; Tuesday, iron seven dozens of clothes. There are things she must do every day, such as clean the bathrooms, wash the floors, wash the dishes, dust the furniture, wash clothes, make the beds, and cook.

Lina is pleased to see the girl go to the TV room and sprawl out on the floor with her legs crossed. She spreads books and notebooks out on the floor, takes an orange pencil, pink pencil, an eraser, and a pencil sharpener in the form of heart out of her pouch. Lina likes to watch her while folding the man's underwear in four parts. She smooths his pants with the iron, separates the shirts, and makes a ball with the socks. It is the best part of her day. The excitement starts from cleaning the last corner of the kitchen, then she flies through the laundry basket and settles in front of the TV. She waits for the girl to turn it on, lie on her belly, start writing, suck a finger, and hum the lyrics while squeezing the pencil...

She works to iron the man's pants flat when she feels something that creeps on her forehead: the girl's greenish eyes that stare at her *if you want, I'll show you, let's play I'm the teacher.* From that day on she hurries, praying the folds are even and the pants don't wrinkle. Her eyes go to the round letter that the girl makes with her tight little hand, *the i is like a stick, do you understand?* Yes, she understands, and she is amazed to understand, *the round and fat o, the a has a tail.* She gets so excited and promises the forty-seven pesos in exchange for teaching. After all, Yeya said to *use it for something important* and this is important. The firl quickly calculates how many bags of potatoes, tamarinds and chocolates you can buy with forty-seven pesos. The girl accepts, arrives on time to classes, adopts a scolding teacher pose, and does what she wants with her student. Lina doesn't care.

Lina gets confused by so much; one afternoon she dares to grab the pencil with her own hands for the first time and without being able to explain it, she knows that she is living a memorable event. Black symbols begin to take shape, although they still don't have meaning.

The girl gets angry at playing the same thing so many afternoons, Lina's stray eyes, the hands she places nervously on her dress, the giggle that indicates she understands nothing. *You are stupid*, she writes her name in a notebook so she can repeat many times to see if she learns. *Take it, I'll give you a pencil.* She runs away and sticks out her tongue.

That night Lina stays up late. She tries to reproduce the round letters of the paper. She wants to show it to the girl, show her that she is not so stupid so she'll feel encouraged to be her teacher again. When she feels she can't anymore, she hears Yeya's comments again through her ears and green courage gets stuck in her throat.

Lina writes the name that the girl has written many times. The white sheets of the notebook are filled with attempts until one night, Lina manages to join a letter with the other *iiii*. She remembers the *nnn*, pronounces the *ddd* with her tongue stuck to her teeth, again *iiii* like a scream and the *aaa.*

She makes a great effort to spell from the beginning iiiiiinnnnnd, iiiinndddi, iinddiia, india. India. India. India. She repeats it many times while looking hypnotized by the name on the paper. She winds the pencil around the sheet, leaves it on the floor, rubs her hands with pleasure, smiles with teeth extremely white on her brown skin and says to herself happily, *damn Yeya, yes, I could, take that!*

A Corvid Story

She used to say she loved me crazily. She liked to emphasize the adverb when the tenderness in her gesture set fire to everything. However, the worst predictions suddenly filtered between us; I guess because the Asian in her was not compatible with my corvid, somewhat dark nature. *But how, Zenaida, how? Are you crazy or what?* Her friends said, he's a common guy, and you're so pretty. She did not pay attention. She had a loving vision of herself: she was capable of being happy with a being like me, so simple, a bird of low intensity capable of making her flutter with pure pleasure. She felt like a warrior for daring to challenge the whole world. Personally, I did not let myself be intimidated by the comments; those of my type are of measured spirit, until they puncture our souls.

I made her crazy (her favorite word) with my strong and long beak. I liked everything about her. We were happy for a while. With the sweetness of those of her species, she knew how to weather the storm, so uneven at times, so rainy at other times. But, to tell the truth, that made her look more distinguished. Now, with my eyes wide open and far from her beauty obscuring my vision, I see the situation clearly: being with me gave her royalty; just as those who live among the dwarves believe themselves to be very tall, my insignificance made her powerful, immortal, the most elegant of all the birds of the region.

As expected, her singing fascinated others, and she let herself get carried away, becoming the innocent pigeon without realizing it. There were several times when I surprised her by flapping my wings to attract attention, cooing at whoever crossed her in front, even a sweet and sleepy pigeon. I did not care so much; she was seductive in nature, but she loved me and only I lit the blue rings that circled her eyes.

She bragged about, among many other things, her gringo descent; she would tell here and there a version of her origin that was difficult to verify, but with such a gurgling that there was no suspicion. With a poise cemented in high-flying cosmopolitan stories, she imbibed everyone and made me a languid of dark wings: at her command and at her disposal. With everything and this, my reason of being was to give her pleasure, making her feel at home, even if her species was miles away from mine. She liked to communicate in a gringo tone with me, especially in public. My legs trembled just imagining myself in a ridiculous situation, becoming unworthy in her eyes. But stoicism is on the side of common males like me, born in the image of the defender. It took some work, but I pretended it was the easiest thing was the world; anything so that she wouldn't find out about the battle she waged with that devil language. Being bilingual wasn't the most shameful thing I did, I also made the terrible mistake of believing in her: in her love and her selflessness, when she said she loved my crow-like appearance, she'd melt — another word she liked — before my very presence.

When the rumors reached me, I flew around like an aimless bird, not knowing what to do or where to direct my wings. I confronted her and she praised me with the same; faced with the falseness of her trickery, my fiery peak flickered in the abyss of her pupils. In front of my iridescent reflection, I imagined caw at those of my class, in a common chorus, *there are many like her, send her to fly away*. I grew up with the idea, I reached a wingspan (the most liked word among my kind) of dimensions never seen; I almost covered the horizon with the width, my unusual power. I felt very macho, I admit it, but I never felt so determined. I stalked her from the window, hidden behind the parapet, ready to unravel my doubts or confirm infamy. I saw her perch at the foot of the stream, dip her red legs in the water, and observe with some relish the most beautiful specimens that used to roam around at that time. She amused herself, I could see from my hiding place, with the Greater Roadrunner or the Boat-billed flycatcher, which lately occupied the best sites of social spectacle. Guessing turned me on more. I lost judgment. Seeing her excited by others led me to lose the scant sanity I had then. How could I fly so low? I started to follow very closely. I adjusted to their flights with caution, with just enough caution to not fall into useless amorous exhibitions: those preferred by the idlers who await public news. My eyes captured an unforgettable aerial shot, which still shakes my crow heart: Zenaida is not one of those who remain hungry. A somewhat insignificant hawfinch awaited her on the edge of a branch. Those who are like me can understand it: I reacted in my inner turmoil; I swallowed my anger in that moment to not miss any details. My feathers bristled like the back of a cat or that of a panther when it perceives the moment to jump over its prey. I wanted to be crucified, pierced by a spear. There was Zenaida, the infidel, the perverse one. My keen vision and my attempts to reach her weren't good enough; she didn't give a damn about my unconditional love. She did not even think for a second about the time we shared. With eagerness to suffer, I observed the whole scene: the hawfinch and my Zenaida, my Zenaida and the hawfinch.

Then I got encouraged: I was too good at being submissive. The hawfinch had been the drop that made the glass overflow and spill. When I arrived, the traitor drank in sips and thought, perhaps, of her exuberant fantasies of palms and flowers, combined with pecks of the damn hawfinch. Very dreamy, right? *Zenaida, this is as far as we go. Are you so conceited over your skinny legs?* She became a turtledove. She tried to convince me with certain oriental curls that used to melt me before (I was determined to steal her little words), but my wings covered her completely, in a kind of shadow. Surely then she had evidence of the deep darkness of which I am capable when they provoke me. By the bristling of the feathers on her forehead, I could see that she was frightened. I liked being the one who had control of the situation. I approached her as much as I could; I felt her tremble, and even so, she didn't lose her queen-like style. I liked it better: my tail was ruffled by the aspiration of her fear. But the curse was cast; and the damage, scattered in fine particles upon us. Her throat lasted a few seconds; I pecked once but before I made sure she heard my two final words, those of farewell, in a raucous squawk that reached every corner: *nunca más, Zenaida.* Since she looked surprised, I told her in the language she liked the most: *never again.* Once her sentence was pronounced, I sank my beak into her beautiful throbbing neck. I still have the sweet taste of her blood in my mouth, and sometimes it makes me sad, but I get over it quickly when I remember her affair with the hawfinch. I no longer fly through those places we shared; I plan for other skies in search of a more reliable bird. Maybe I'll find a simpler and less into herself kind of girl; a corvid that is satisfied with me and does not need to give airs of greatness with other beaks.

Blackish Green

The garden was lush. Sparkling, that was the word. Bernardo found it quite cheesy. Marcela tried to dissuade him because it was still too early to fight and the sun would soon stop coloring the patio tiles. They just arrived and had barely unpacked the backpacks in the room just as they usually do. She played some word games dealing with the art of sparkling, then she wanted to caress back of his neck and say: I sparkle, you sparkle, let's make all of this sparkle. Bernardo thought verbs were something else. She tickled his ears with her fingers and played with his eardrum using her tongue. Anyone would say that they both thought at the same time: they took the cobbled path to reach room 208. Their shadows traveled, section by section, the round surface of the stones. His walk showed indifference: one hand in his pocket and the other holding his phone. *Laziness kills me, oh baby, it tears me apart.* Since they left the city, he had the lyrics of the song sewn to his body and sang it in a low voice. *Tarareas, tara, tarado,* chanted Marcela.

The brochure said that the men of the house decided to make the wasteland green again, considering the space had become barren due to lack of care as years passed. A family history from the sixties was plastered on all four sides of the promotional material, made of steely paper. She read it completely; him, just some lines. In a very beautiful poetic prose, Marcela commented, there it's said that there is no garden that resists oblivion, and the men were very sorry to look out the window of their room; they ended up closing it and only opening it in cases of extreme need, but they realized that it was easier to take care of that horrendous wasteland and return its vitality to it by cloaking it in stone and mud.

Overnight, the illusion caught their souls and they did not stop until they out the most exotic plants in the region in the garden. *They hang from the branches*, Bernardo noted, wanting to indicate the exaggeration of the expression. *In this town you can hardly see some orange trees and some fucking discolored weeds.* And they did it: since their children were grown, the garden was the important thing. They put acacias, nopals, a couple of slender trees called *izotes*, with a thorn at the tip and very sharp leaves. It was vital to brag to visitors how good and unique the place was. But it was not enough. Excited with the change of landscape from their window, they ordered a cyclone net and released multicolored birds into the garden, brought from various parts of the country. They were careful with the choice: they had to be of similar species so that they did not peck each other and so they could reproduce easily. That's what the brochure said. Marcela read it carefully. *Don't fuck around, it isn't even that interesting.* When he said this, she had finished reading. *I hate romantic stories.* Upon hearing it, Marcela got involved in reading something else from the beginning and tried to read it much slower.

Maybe that's why he came up with the word. They had barely gotten out of the Jeep when a bird with a sparkling tail perched on a branch. From then on, he had to discuss the childishness of that word's origins until they started walking down the stone path. It was the same path that the gentlemen made to easily connect the garden with the rooms of the house. They walked in silence, with some solemnity, as if it were a case of life or death. *Do not sing, do not sing.* And he sang. *Laziness kills me...*

It was a simple room: the necessities, no ostentation. When she left the bathroom, she found him sitting at the edge of the bed, making a gesture that had to do with the verbs stick it in, take it out, thrust. Since his childhood, Bernardo was a fan of verbs. This wasn't obvious, but he did make a mention of how much the immobility of nouns bored him. Every time someone insisted on speaking without action, he interrupted with a frantic *so what happened?* Assemble was a good verb. A bit technical, yes. That's what Marcela thought when she got on her legs and had him face to face: in electronic parts or gears. She introduced herself slowly, with hip movements. When he put his hands on her butt and urged her to move in a more rhythmic and sustained way, she thought about puzzle pieces and was turned on by the idea that every piece has its counterpart. He took off her blouse. Marcela remembered a game of putting together a puzzle one Christmas. She played it so much that she knew by heart what piece went with which. Bernardo licked her breasts, the right one more than the left, then took them by the ends, as if he wanted to join them, inflate them into a single udder, *tell me to milk you.* Recently Marcela had learned that olive trees are also milked; while he squeezed her nipples, she imagined those hands sliding down the branch, looking for an olive to bite it and devour its green flesh. He raised his face and looked for her eyes. She brushed her hair aside and imagined that tiny but sharp teeth were around her neck. People hated bats because of evil legends and the abundant fiction written about them, but in reality, the white-winged vampire bat is almost a bird. The men had never thought of having winged mammals. One night, they were struck by the vision of a very white and bright cloud elegantly flying over the greenery and decided to respect its presence in the garden. This, since it is already known, was not stated in the brochure; the manager was in charge of telling them the story while taking guests' data and assigning the room. Bernardo squeezed her butt, bit her arms, urged her to move faster. Putting a one piece next to another was easy, the complicated thing was to find them. The colors said it all: the green ones went with the green ones, the black ones with the black ones. He thrusted in and out, kneeled on the bed and pounded until he climaxed. Her reaction was more of a shriek, sharp enough to clash with his hoarse groan. Lying in bed,

Marcela was struck by the idea that a bunch of bats watched them from the garden.

From a plastic card on the nightstand they got the room service number. He opened a small bottle of whiskey and, with the sign of her approval, served two on the rocks. When the chips and sandwiches arrived, Marcela was amazed. When she opened the door, she saw that the night had eaten everything. Bats committed scandals at night and the birds did theirs during the day. That's what they said. She looked for the bats among the fragments of garden already covered by darkness and it was difficult to distinguish them; the languid light from the lanterns was insufficient.

In bed again, Marcela wanted to talk, she wanted a flock of words to fall on them and get between their legs, between their toes, behind their ears. To look for them until all of them are found and they fall defeated between them, side by side. *Don't fuck with me*, Bernardo said for the second time lying in bed, *that's just cheesy bullshit. Flocks of words don't exist.* Marcela ignored the comment and formed as many images as she could with her words: she apologized, stacked them like her puzzle pieces and resumed the game. *Salgamos a cortar centellas. Laziness kills me, oh baby, it tears me apart.* She was thinking of starting with the *tara y tarado* chant when she fell asleep, still with the jingle in her mind. He turned on the television. He served himself another whiskey. Marcela slept at the bottom of the well, as she liked to say. He did not understand; it had never occurred to him to relate deep sleep with a coin that spins in the air until it sinks to the bottom. Time cannot be specified, but we can deduce that he had spent at most an hour, when she felt, from the depth of the well, his hands, searching, finding. Fucking was not one of her words. She was not in the mood to be fucked while she slept. She liked to feel fucked, in the rural sense of receiving him and vice versa, like the land to water. She said no, without saying a word. She was tired of using so many words, or maybe it was the whiskey, or that the bats would have been another myth of the house, but she no longer wanted to say anything, she just wanted to go to the bottom of that magnificent well. He moved to the rhythm of in, out, thrust, lick. She insisted: *no*, tacitly, just as he liked, without speaking. Turning around was the same as *I want to sleep*. An easy equation to understand.

The following may be expected, but just as the *izotes* sometimes run out of branches, she also ran out of words. Now it is easy to think of the outcome. She resisted as much as she could to open her eyes, but his fingers already opened her vagina, separated her legs and put her on her knees. Already well awake, she was very aware that lying down was the perfect signal for him to understand that "taking from behind" was not her favorite phrase, even less at that moment, when everything had already been swallowed by the night. Again and again: *no* and *no* and *no*. The following actions were so fast that she could no longer react: the strength of his hands on her hips, her knees on the sheets. Dogs fuck from behind, and she was bothered by the scene. As a child they told her it was not good to stop to look because something happens in the tear ducts, a grain breaks out or something. In the final shout, he told her that hated word, the one that seemed most infectious and detestable to her. One, several times, many, until he collapsed beside her and turned on the television again. He commented something about her and her word games, she only heard, along with his snoring, the ringing, thousands of times, of that abhorred word.

When closing the door, the number 208, carved in the wood of the door and covered in gold paint, reminded her again of the flashes. The sound of the crickets in the corners of that blackened garden would not be able to wake anyone. Overhead, she thought she saw an open window and thought of the men of the house watching the burning cloud of white bats. With the backpack on her back, she walked down the cobblestone road and headed for the Jeep. From where she was, everything looked blacker than ever. She kept thinking about it when he started the engine. Bernardo was right. *Centella* was a bad word. It wasn't even about flares or fireflies. Who thought to think that a flock of bats might look like a sparkle? A few languid lanterns. All black. Fuck twinkles. Fucking trees. Fucking blackish green olive meat. Fucking herbs. Fucking word games. Fucking romantic story. Fuck.

Killing

We made the last leg of the journey in silence. We had left around dawn, so maybe it was the tiredness, the dry weather that didn't let heat flow, the scarcity of wind, and the smell of pasture in my nose. I got impatient and when that happens my legs and arms cramp up, it's as if I didn't fit in my available space. At first, I had thought about the possibility of traveling as something joyful or exciting to shake up my routine; now, with Nicolás immersed in a silence like mine, I was not so sure. I carried the box with his brothers' gift on my legs: a legion of plastic superheroes, all of identical size.

Suddenly, as if emerging from nowhere, we saw a stocky, generous oak tree. It was the welcome sign, Nicolás had already told me. The house was nestled in the middle of an arid mountain, a desolate wilderness where *huizaches* were barely distinguishable from the terrified run of a squirrel or a rabbit. We got out of the car. The autumn leaves creaked under our feet. On the doorstep, like in a country movie, the whole family was ready to welcome us. The mother opened her arms as soon as we were a meter away. She squeezed Nicolás in a long hug, as she said in his ear how much she had missed him all this time.

I have always found introductions cumbersome. I never know what to say or how to conduct myself, especially in cases like this, in which Nicolás's mother seemed to be too restless about her son's relationship with me. I answered without evasion, but with short answers, with the intention of avoiding saying something that I could later regret. The children also asked questions but weren't very interested in personal matters. Instead, they all questioned at once: What did they bring us? How many hours did they travel? Those kinds of things.

All of them, as if bound by an indissoluble bond, led us to meet the pig. Although there were others in the pen, it was very easy to identify. It was a huge animal with a round body, long snout and four fingers on each leg. He rubbed himself with the others as he moved across the floor, obviously slippery, of mud and waste. There was some dignity in his brown eyes, which I approached struck by the curiosity of finding something in the meek pupils of a death row inmate. Nothing. My gaze sank into that imperturbable abyss. All together again, they pulled him out of there and placed him in a small circle surrounded by wire. Between grunts, he seemed to oppose being taken out of his space. They explained to me that the pig had to abstain from eating several hours before the event, so they had to isolate him and clean his new dwelling frequently.

His mom asked if we were hungry, although she did it only looking at Nicolás, who answered for both of us. We had sausage with potatoes and pineapple atole. I was fascinated by the inflated tortillas on the griddle and the skill with which Nicolás's mother was had flipped them, achieving an even heating. A fleeting moment of bliss filled the atmosphere, by work and grace of those bodies of mass that were transformed by the effect of heat. I felt that Nicolás was the guy from the city again, the one in the little room above the restaurant, with diamond-shaped pajamas and bare feet. When I finished, I wanted to clean myself up but his mother stopped me with a sweeping, forceful gesture.

Nicolás and I went for a walk towards the stream. A squirrel came out to us and when it sensed our presence, it disappeared. It was a gentle creek, with a rather low water level. We talked a little about country life, while we gathered languid branches that floated on the surface and then put them on the shore. When we finally got to a certain dialogue, he felt a tickle in one ear. He searched with his little finger without success, then I dug into it carefully, also without locating anything. I made some jokes about it with the intention of breaking the ice, but the sensation of tiny wings in continuous rubbing with his ear canal made him nervous.

When we entered, his mother sharpened the knife and the children played with the superhero figures on the floor. Nicolás, with the anguish of a small child who has scratched his knee, explained the insect in his ear incident. Then, they gave each other a look that seemed to be enough. As if they had already done it so many times, they sat down in the chairs next to each other. He laid his head on her legs and closed his eyes. I tried to follow the childrens' game, but something made me turn and see. The mother parted her hair from her forehead, made and undid some curls with her fingers, blew into the invaded ear causing Nicolás an unknown, strange giggle; when they got the animal, they both laughed in a regular rhythm for a while. Then they stayed in the same posture: her mouth in his ear, whispering, and he remained in in her lap. I deduced that it was not common talk between mother and child, however, communication flowed with agility between specific codes and signs. From a long time ago, I thought.

On the table were several plastic containers. A huge pot occupied the four burners of the stove. Leftovers from breakfast had been removed. I was about to sit down when, with the gesture from his mother, Nicolás took the containers and called us all to the field. Without his mother in between, each of the children ran out and only when we were in front of the pig did they swirl around it, their faces glued to the mesh. I knew the time had come.

I was so engrossed with the pig, I hadn't realized when Nicolás's mother arrived. The children surrounded her, as if they were about to ask for permission or concession. She carried a bag made of jute, where I saw the handle of a knife, ropes, various utensils, the tip of a bottle of aguardiente. She poured three glasses and ordered us, again with her eyes only on Nicolas, to drink with only one gulp. After serving herself and drinking several times, she cleared her throat for a long time, spit and faced her gaze to the pig's, whose eyes looked fainter than ever.

She assigned a plastic bucket to everyone. I tried to look for a certain contact in Nicolás and took his hand as in a kind of solidarity act, contaminated with tints of death. Without strength, he let me hold his hand for a few seconds, then dropped mine. The pig looked nowhere; he shook his nose and his snout to scare off some flies that roamed around him and spread on the ground. I imagined the inside of that huge body: guts in motion, hot organs, blood. A jet spouted at the first picket, killed by the mother's firm hand. The pig burst, literally, in exorbitant shrieks, out of every auditory limitation. The first was a long shriek, so long that it could have been the only one, but others followed, for a long time.

I left the group and went to the house without excusing myself. As much as I closed the door and the windows, the sharp shrieks of the pig invaded every inch of the place. I sat in an armchair to wait for time to pass so I could leave as soon as possible. I started counting the seconds on my watch, then the minutes. At a screech from the mother I ran, without thinking, where the blood of the pig continued to flow, I located my plastic container and placed it in one of the many dumps. The children looked happy, bright in that macabre scene in the middle of the forest. Nicolás and his mother worked at a perfect pace, they understood each other even without speaking, with simple movements or signs.

A while later, I took a bath and put on a white dress lined with lace on the shoulders and the skirt; I had chosen it precisely for the occasion since Nicolás invited me to meet his family, distracting ourselves with the purity of the countryside. The presence of the pig invaded everything. I even came to recognize it in the intense smell that my skin gave off after bathing. From the window of the room, I saw two huge pots that the children had placed in the center of the field. Nicolás helped his mother to accommodate the tables and chairs. I waved my hand as if we hadn't seen each other for a long time.

The party started at twelve o'clock on the dot. Dozens of people took their places and everything was filled with excitement and movement. Men and women peeked into cauldrons, rubbed their hands, and made jokes. I stayed with the children the entire time while Nicolás helped his mother with the guests. I was nervous and watched the pig pen the whole time, especially the empty enclosure, as if from one moment to another the pig inhabited it again. The boiling of the blood in butter abruptly entered me and I felt that it stayed forever, attached to my ribs and my belly. I thought that the wind and the people would blur the image of the pig: it was the exact opposite. It was everywhere.

I helped as much as I could, especially with arrangement of cutlery and plates. I was in the kitchen, counting equal amounts of knives, forks and spoons, when Nicolás entered, accompanied by his mother. They were engaged in a conversation where it was difficult to extract the essential content. They went to the pot on the stove, where the pig's head boiled between spices and condiments. Then the mother, at Nicolás's attentive gaze, said something of cooking it evenly, then immediately took the head by the ears, reversed its arrangement and tried to immerse it again in the boiling broth.

The shrieks erupted with such force that Nicolás ran for advice to remedy the growing pain. The guests came to see what was happening. Some suggested manure paste; others, clove crushed with vinegar; there were even those who recommended covering the burns with fresh milk, to mitigate the affected areas.

The presence of the pig blurred with the fall of the afternoon. The party ended much earlier than expected, but sometimes that's how it goes when unexpected things happen. The bed got big that night; Nicolás told me that he should stay with his mother, that I would surely understand him. The children took a long time to fall asleep – I heard them fight with their dolls – perhaps riled up by the latest events. It also seemed too late for me. A sweet sleepiness began to invade me, despite the shrieks combined with the comforting voice of Nicholas. I dreamt of a gigantic pig, happy in his universe of mud and waste. After a long time, the shrieks subsided. Finally, the peaceful silence of the countryside covered everything.

INDEX

La Pereza Ediciones, Corp
Also Publishes

The narrative construction and the characters of Acevedo, are not supposed to conform to the norms. Time in some cases swing back and forth, the present can be past, and some rememberings can exist in a extravagant nostalgia.

Night Has Fallen Here tells the story of André, a sullen man in his early thirties who returns to Mexico City after having lived abroad for almost a decade. Broke and feeling profoundly estranged from the world around him, he moves back in with his mother and attempts to rebuild his life from scratch. He embarks on a quest to find his place in the world, delving into his past, building new relationships, and wandering, tirelessly, through a city that both repulses and fascinates him. His mother, meanwhile, struggles to cope with her son's unsettling transformation and growing isolation; he has come back to her after all these years, but as a stranger suffering from an affliction she is powerless to assuage.

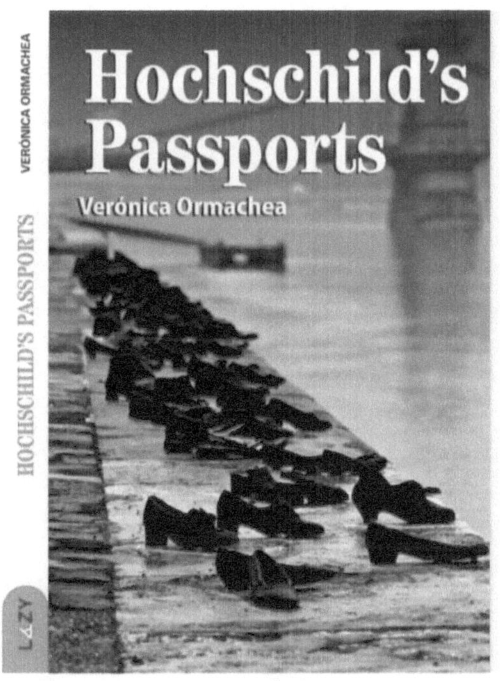

"Throughout the novel's almost three hundred pages, Verónica Ormachea takes us on a journey through time and space to the broken heart of the twentieth century, via a fast-paced and skillfully narrated story. From the persecution of the Jews in Warsaw to the horrors of Auschwitz, from the heights of La Paz to the rooms of the Waldorf Astoria in New York or the Dorchester in London, her characters are embroiled in conflicts that bring both their contradictions and their greatness to light—as in the case of Moritz Hochschild, a genuine Bolivian Schindler."—Javier Moro, Spanish writer, winner of the Premio Planeta de Novela (2011)

THE RUINS

Rafael Reyes-Ruiz

"Cosmopolitan in the best sense of the word, The Ruins is part genealogical search, part star-crossed romance, part ethnographic encounter, fused together in a spellbinding mystery that circumnavigates the globe. Reyes-Ruiz combines the trained eye of the anthropologist with the imagination of a seasoned novelist, managing to be learned and accessible at the same time. Highly recommended."

Peter Kalliney, William J. Tuggle Chair in English at the University of Kentucky.